COMING OUT
mikala

sylvia aguilar-zéleny

EPIC
Press

Mikala
Coming Out: Book #2

Written by Sylvia Aguilar-Zéleny

Copyright © 2016 by Abdo Consulting Group, Inc.

Published by EPIC Press™
PO Box 398166
Minneapolis, MN 55439

Cover design by Nicole Ramsay
Images for cover art obtained from Shutterstock.com
Edited by Nancy Cortelyou

LIBRARY OF CONGRESS CATALOGING-IN-PUBLICATION DATA

Aguilar-Zéleny, Sylvia.
Mikala / Sylvia Aguilar-Zéleny.
p. cm. — (Coming out)
Summary: Mikala's grandparents are the traditional type whose beliefs are against her
real lifestyle, being a lesbian. Having to lie to the only family she has, Mikala's life
changes forever after a visit with her best friend to the Big Apple.
ISBN 978-1-68076-011-8 (hardcover)
1. Homosexuality—Fiction. 2. Lesbians—Fiction. 3. Lesbian teenagers—Fiction.
4. Coming out (Sexual orientation)—Fiction. 5. Young adult fiction. I. Title.
[Fic]—dc23
2015932733

EPIC
Press

EPICPRESS.COM

To those who follow their hearts
no matter who, no matter what

CHAPTER ONE
born queer

JANUARY 1ST

Hi, there. Happy New Year!

My name is Mikala Kekoa. I am seventeen years old and I am queer. You *do* know what queer is, right? Well, in case you have lived in a basement for the last fifteen years, or your grandparents, parents, friends, church, or the entire society has kept you in the dark, I will explain to you what queer means.

Queer used to be a word to insult people who were either gay, lesbian, bisexual, or transgender. I guess it can still be an insult, depending on how you use it. But if you're queer, meaning, if you are gay, lesbian, bisexual or transgender, you can call yourself queer, and no, it would not be an insult. Calling yourself queer is like *owning* who you are.

Anyway, the reason I'm telling you I'm queer is because if you a) don't know the term, or b) you hate the term because you are a homophobic son of a bitch, then this is the moment when you must close this notebook, leave it where you found it, and disappear.

BUT, if a) you still don't understand the term, but you are curious to learn, or b) you do know the term, or c) you embrace it, either because you are queer or queer friendly, then, welcome to my diary.

If you are reading this, it means that I have accomplished my goal, and I am in Hawaii. It also means that I was able to pack this diary in one plastic bag after another and throw it in the sea, so it could travel and travel and travel until you picked it up somewhere on the Pacific coast. Or maybe I just left it on a bus, a ferry, or the subway and you found it there.

Anyway . . .

I wonder what made you take this thing? I wonder what made you open it? I wonder what day, month, year it is now? I wonder if you will continue reading it? I wonder who you are, as I am sure you wonder who the hell I am. One thing I can tell you is that destiny has brought us together. I know I'm young, and even though I have no clue who you are or how old you are, there is a chance I can teach you a thing or two about being queer.

So, how are you? Take a minute and tell yourself how you feel. Imagine you are telling me about it. Tell me something about you, and then if you are up for it, I can tell you about me, about how I was born queer and how I have forced myself to live in the closet even though I have these wonderful fantasies of being out and being the biggest lesbian in the world. If you wanna read about me, *E komo mai!* Welcome, come in!

JANUARY 2ND

Where were we? Let's see, I already told you that my name is Mikala. Did I mention it's Hawaiian? It means gift from God. So you should

7

look at me with my ribbon and everything. I am such a gift (but ungifted because I don't draw, paint, sing or play any instrument). I am Hawaiian, or sorta. My mother and both my grandparents are Hawaiian. I was born in Honolulu, but was brought to the mainland when I was very little (remind me to tell you about this story, it's kinda creepy but, oh well). I have never been back to Hawaii (isn't that horrible?) and I dream, dream, dream of doing so.

I don't know exactly how it has worked for the rest of the queer people in the world, but as for me, I believe I was born queer because there are some *Māhū* genes in me. In Hawaii there were people called *Māhū*, and the *Māhū* often did whatever they wanted in terms of gender. What I mean is that they were a little bit trans—girls would act like boys and nobody cared that they sometimes had *aikāne*, which means same-sex relationships (and if you ask me, I think *aikāne* rules).

So, as I was saying, the *Māhū* were highly respected, nobody messed with them (unlike every place in the world these days. I mean, think of all the drama a family experiences these days when their kid comes out of the closet). Going back in time, the *Māhū* were even considered the healers of society. I like thinking that this was because they were able to give the same love to a woman or to a man.

I'm not saying that I'm a real *Māhū*, but I think something *Māhū*-ish is in my blood, because I have always felt I could act and be like a boy or like a girl. So, I thought I was bisexual for a while—I thought I liked boys AND girls. I even went through a very tomboyish period (which Grandma hated to the point that she stopped talking to me for almost a month). But back to my story. There was a point in my life that I thought I might be *trans*, you know a girl who actually wants to be a boy. After reading and watching testimonies of some trans teens, I learned that no, I wasn't trans. I came to the conclusion that I liked boobs, mine and others, and I didn't want a dick (although being with a girl and using, ahem, a plastic, ahem, dick, ahem, doesn't sound too bad. Am I embarrassing you, Reader? I am embarrassing myself, I think).

There's no trapped boy inside of me dying to get out. No, not at all. I am just a girl who happens to like girls, all types: tall, short, blonde, brunette, girls with glasses, girls with braces, girls playing chess or playing soccer. Just gimme girls and I will like them!

Do I make any sense? Your options are: a) Yes, b) Kinda, c) Not at all.

JANUARY 2ND AFTERNOON

I've been re-reading my last two pages and I can see that you know a couple of things about me, but there's so much more I can still tell you. Where do I start?

OK, I know, I can start by telling you that I live in New Jersey (which I kinda hate because even though it is very close to NYC it is definitely not NYC). (All New Jersey residents feel the same frustration I do—about being so close, but yet so far, although I doubt many admit it.) New Jersey kinda sucks, but we don't talk about it, it's like the elephant walking around our houses and farting on our noses. You see, even though there's a very energetic queer scene in New Jersey, well, I can't really be a part of it because my grandparents would find out. I mean they're not gay haters or anything like that, it's just that they've been through too much shit as parents, so I don't wanna load them with more shit. Oh, yeah, I haven't told you this, I live with them.

My grandparents are Mr. and Mrs. Kekoa. My grandpa's name is Haku, which means "supervisor" or "overseer." My grandma's name is Ailani, which means "high chief." Isn't it funny? (Deep inside I think that they got together because their names required them to merge, as if they were companies.) So, the names suit them. Both of them are kinda bossy, but they are also very, very caring and loving.

My grandparents have raised me my whole life. They even gave me their last name. They have always provided me with everything and anything

I have needed. They are great. I sometimes dream that one day I'll come out and they will be happy and accepting and walk in the Gay Pride parade with me. But it's just a dream, I don't think a) I will ever dare to come out, and b) if I did, they would not be parading around, celebrating it.

But they are cool, believe me. You might think they are not cool, considering I have to hide my queerness from them. (Geez, you should see them, asking me if I like someone, asking me not to hide from them if I'm dating some good boy. And you should see them completely ignorant that their granddaughter drools for a good pair of legs and boobs.) What you gotta understand is that they are very traditional, you know, they are capital-letter, old fashioned font Traditional.

Sometimes I think that it's like they've never left the island, even though they detest the island. They *are* an island in so many ways. For example, they don't have friends who are not Hawaiian or at least some kind of Pacific Islander. They are closed-minded, I guess. I don't know, I can't explain it very well, it just feels like our home is an island floating all alone in the middle of our neighborhood.

Also, they can be very strict, but I know it's because they care and worry about me. They want me to be happy and succeed in life. They don't want me to end up like Luana.

Believe me, I don't wanna end up like Luana.

Luana is my mother, only I don't call her Mom. Why? Because she is far from being a mother. Don't get me wrong, it's not like I don't love her, I do (the same way you would love a crazy older sister or a crazy aunt, or just a crazy woman who happens to be in your family).

Luana was born in the '70s and she lived during the boom of Hawaii in the '80s, and then the bust in the '90s. In case you don't know, during these years the island became *the* place, it became a paradise for tourism, and surfing. It was C R A Z Y, or so I've heard. Luana not only lived off that craziness, she *became* the craziness of Hawaii in those years.

Grandma says Luana started hitching when she was in high school. Then they started losing track of Luana for days, DAYS, until she finally came back home broke, drunk, or high. Sometimes she would bring along a new boyfriend, some surfer from a faraway place. "She would always come back with the face of a woman who had surfed a tsunami and barely survived," Grandma would say. (Grandpa believes that there was probably a mix of vodka and rum in those tsunamis Luana surfed.)

Anyway, one time, after weeks and weeks of being gone, Luana came back, as broke as always, only this time she wasn't drunk or high, just pregnant. Very pregnant. Pregnant with me, little Mikala who was just a little seed in her belly. Mr. and Mrs. Kekoa were obviously disappointed with their only child, but both of them thought that maybe it wasn't all so bad; maybe a baby would ground Luana.

That's the other side of my grandparents. They can be so optimistic, and so, so naïve. Or at least they were naïve with her that one time. One thing you can't deny is that my grandparents are tender, and good-hearted, so obviously they helped her out. Luana is their only daughter, after all. They got her an apartment and offered her a monthly allowance. In their minds, Luana's new baby was going to make her grow up. They were sure that things would change for good.

Only they didn't. At all. Nothing changed. Things got a lot worse in Luana's life. The baby, meaning ME, did not make her grow up.

Oh, wait, I'm making you sad, aren't I? Let's save that story of how my grandparents rescued me from crazy Luana for later because now there are more important things to talk about. For example, this diary.

You're probably wondering why I wrote it and why are you reading it. So let's start with that. (Wait no, you'll have to wait because now it's time for dinner and I have to set the table, prepare the juice, and get cleaned up, not in that order of course.)

JANUARY 14TH

I have been too busy to write in my diary, but you probably didn't notice because you're just reading page after page. How does it feel to read someone else's diary? Do you feel naughty? Ha, ha. (And I haven't even written to you about sex. Because of course I have like zero experience with sex.)

The truth is I had always believed diaries were dumb and cheesy. If you think what you have read so far is dumb and cheesy, you have two options, a) leave this where you found it and have a happy life, or b) continue reading because, hey, this is my first diary so maybe it starts off dumb and cheesy, but it will get better.

As I was saying, I didn't believe in diaries. I thought diaries were for damsels in distress or some shit like that, but my friend Soledad convinced me that I have a gift. Sole thinks I should become a playwright, a screenwriter, or at least a copywriter like those characters in *Mad Men*.

Soledad says that the only way to become a good writer, no matter what the genre, is by writing every single day. Soledad is pretty smart herself. At least sometimes. At least when there's no alcohol involved. At least when there are no cute girls or handsome boys around. Remind me to tell you about that later.

I have to confess that she told me this, you know, about having to write, one time when I was crying my ass off because being a queer girl, a queer closet girl, is hard. Even harder? Being a queer closet only child girl. I was opening up to Soledad, telling her how sometimes I felt fake in front of my grandparents, even in front of the mirror. "I am a fake image of myself," I said.

Sole was like, "Whoa, dude that is a beautiful line, you should write it down."

I did. I started writing down the phrases that Soledad found interesting, phrases like:

- *Sometimes it's better not to know everything about everybody.*

- *I am a coloring outside of the lines kinda girl.*
- *Sadness? You gotta learn to keep it in your pocket.*
- *My sex education came from seeing Bert and Ernie living together.*

Then, little by little, I kept a record of phrases that came to my mind and that *I* liked. Once I had a long list, I shared it with her. This was last year, and from time to time, Sole read my words. Then, one day, she told me, "You can be in the queer closet as much as you want, but you are a writer. You can't be in the writer's closet any longer."

I was like, "So what should I do?"

Soledad looked at me with her big black eyes and her thick black eyebrows and said, "Well, write, duh!" I told her I couldn't do that, I wouldn't know where to start and she said, "Well, write a diary, start with that."

I said, "No way."

She said, "Yes way."

Then you know how during the holidays

everybody starts planning their New Year's resolutions? I did too; writing this diary became my resolution.

So not only did she convince me to write a diary, but also to take Creative Writing as an elective with Miss Moore. Sole says she's great. We'll see, classes just started. Soledad says that with Miss Moore, I will be writing all the time. "She comes up with great prompts and exercises. Hers is like the best elective ever." (Which makes me wonder how she failed last semester.)

So, the idea of this diary is to obviously write about me, about what I want, about who I am. I wanna write entries that can help me understand myself and maybe help others understand themselves. I'm not quoting Sole, just so you know. Most likely she said something like, "Just fucking write Mikala, pull it all out."

Soledad is the kind of crazy that you end up understanding. She is my best friend, and before I continue explaining to you about this diary, let me tell you about her.

Story of How I Met Soledad and How We Became Friends

I met Soledad like two years ago, when she moved here. She was the mysterious olive-skinned new student at Jefferson High. She has lived in many places. She is half-Spanish, half-gypsy, half-German. (Wait, those are too many halves, aren't they?) What I'm trying to say is that she's a mixture of places and people. I liked her since the first moment I saw her. I knew I wanted to become friends with her. I can't explain—it's like when you go to a store and see a pair of tennis shoes and you know those are the ones for you. Soledad was the one for me. And I have sorta become the one for her. No, no, no, there's nothing between us, we are just friends, buddies, BFFs. Although, she can get so jealous about me hanging out with other people that sometimes I think we are one of those old couples who love each other—like we're too lazy to have sex, but still can't let go. We're like the female version of Ernie and Bert, arguing all the time, but together all the time.

I don't remember who started talking to who, but I do remember we were in PE class, trying to ignore the fact that no one was choosing us for their volleyball team. We ended up making fun of ourselves. What else was there to do? We started talking there, and then continued our conversation in the showers. Next thing I knew we were having smoothies at King's and lattés at Starbucks.

Soledad came out to me in a very straightforward way.

Me: So, what do you like, what do you do when you're in school?

Soledad: I like girls, I like boys. I'm bi. And I argue with my parents about stupid shit as a hobby. You?

I was like, "Oh, shit." My face blushed, my whole

body entered into this warm space I can't describe. I didn't know what to say at first. I nodded, I think, yes, I nodded as if she had just told me she likes both café mochas and vanilla almond cappuccinos. I thought about it for a second, and then decided to find out more about her.

Me: So, are you really bisexual?

Soledad: Yes.

Me: Wow.

Soledad: Wow? Come on, I don't know what the big deal is, really. The way I see it, we are ALL bisexuals until the contrary is proven.

Me: The contrary?

Soledad: Yes, until someone comes and shoots in your heart so hard that you realize that you are gay, super gay, hetero, or super hetero. Does that make sense?

Me: Kinda.

Soledad: Have you ever considered shaving your hair, like only on one side? It'd look cool, it will fit your bob and your bangs. You have such great hair: black, thick, straight.

Yeah, Soledad adds a few drops of fashion onto her philosophy plate. She can discuss being agnostic (which I still don't exactly understand) while at the same time find you a good pair of shades. But back to my story, I didn't come out to her then. It took me longer to open up. She claims she knew it, but Soledad claims many things. For example, she says that if I tried to make friends with her it was just because I liked her, she says my gaydar started buzzing when I saw her. I keep telling her no, but she can't believe I didn't have a crush on her the minute I saw her. (Oh, my friend and her ego.)

Soledad is the one who taught me about the *queer* concept. We were talking about people in our school, she said she felt there were many more queers around us than I imagined.

Me: Queer?

Soledad: Queer. Yes, being *queer* is being like you and me. You know, people who believe in free love, people who don't believe in genders. I don't believe in genders, all I see are human beings.

Soledad's Definition of Queer:

"Look Mikala, queer is a person who simply feels his or her identity doesn't fit or follow the 'norms' of society. You need an example? Well, society says that women fall in love with men and they have babies. What society sometimes (very often) almost always forgets is that there are women who fall in love with women, there are men who fall in love with men, and all of them can do scientific or legal stuff to have babies, too. Society (that bitch!) sometimes (very often) almost always ignores that there are men who hate being men and have surgeries to become women. There are also women who dream of being men instead of women. Let's just say that tits and dicks are sometimes misplaced."

All that, dear Reader, is QUEERNESS, according

to my best friend. After hearing what sounded more like a LGBT activist speech, I realized that I was queer. Very queer.

She continued, "I like girls and I like boys. But one thing I can tell you, I don't like Guido girls or Guido boys." That's the thing with Soledad, I tell you. She can be super deep, and then turn into a superficial bitch. Don't worry, I'm not insulting my friend, that's what we call each other. "Bitch." I am her bitch and she is mine.

But back to the story.

When she told me all this, I was frozen for like a million years. Then Soledad started poking me.

Soledad: You OK, girl? Did I scare you?

Me: No, you didn't, it's just . . .

Soledad: WHAT?

Soledad and her big black eyes staring daggers at me.

Me: You don't look like *that kind* of person. You don't look queer.

Soledad: What am I supposed to look like?

Imagine this: she's all tall, like a tree, her hands on her waist, me as short as a hobbit. Believe me, I thought she was gonna slap me.

Me: I dunno.

Soledad: Hey, we need to pluck your eyebrows with these tweezers I just bought.

Me: My eyebrows, why?

Soledad: So you can actually have two and not just one long line. Anyway, I didn't say I was a lesbian, I told you I'm bisexual, I'm queer. Besides, the time when lesbians were big, dark-mustached, angry butches is long gone, girl.

Me: Yeah, I guess.

Soledad: How 'bout you? You like girls or boys, both, or none?

To this day I don't know what got into me. I'm not that open with people I barely know. Without thinking too much about it I said, "I, I think I like girls."

Soledad said, "Wait, you *think* you like girls or

you *like* girls? You have really long eyelashes, has anybody told you that?"

Two things happened that day. I came out to Soledad and I became her fashion experiment. She's been doing makeovers on me again and again. So, to sum things up, my dear Reader, that is how Soledad and I became super BFFs. We started hanging out all the time. We texted all day long, and we spent hours talking on the phone. I think my life can be divided in two:

Before Soledad, B.S. (which I know looks like I'm saying bullshit).

After Soledad, A.S. (which I know that with one more *s* it would be like saying ass).

I'm trying to make things clear to you, Dear Reader, now you know when I tell you an anecdote and I say B.S. you will know that was back when I was a lesbian dork, and when I say A.S. you will know that is now, when I am queer and proud of it.

Time to go to bed. Talk to you tomorrow.

27

January 15TH

Mikala's Phrases of the Week:

- *Pens are for boys, pencils for girls*
- *Memories make you dizzy, or is it the vodka?*
- *Burn bridges or build bridges? That is the freaking question.*
- *The peace brought by the pretty-sweet-round pair of boobs in front of you.*
- *Imaginary girlfriends. I have a couple of those.*

January 15TH Afternoon

Soledad is right, Miss Moore is *da shit*. She is absolutely awesome. Today she was talking to us about Roald Dahl and how he became a writer. You know, the one who wrote *Charlie and the Chocolate Factory* and many, many other stories? She read some excerpts of his autobiography to us and explained to us how he never planned to be a writer, it was something that was within him. He once said that becoming a writer was "pure fluke." That's how I feel (not that I'm comparing myself to Mr. Dahl, of course). Lately, I have realized that I do have a need to tell stories, but the fact that I met Sole and she encouraged me to do it, that's the "pure fluke" part.

So I started thinking that if I do become a writer, there are two books I know I want to write. One is about discovering Hawaii as a Hawaiian. It will kind of be my own way to discover the island where I was born, and that intrigues me so much. The other one would not be as deep, you will laugh probably but I wanna write a book about Soledad. She is such a character, you can't deny it. You don't know her, Reader, but I know you're already hooked on her. And I haven't even told you half of the things I know about her.

Soledad has such a big personality that it took me a while before I decided to invite her home. You see, although I was fond of her I wasn't all that sure about how my grandparents would feel about her. But Sole is a great actress, and she knew exactly how to perform the role of the nice friend of the nice granddaughter.

But she deserves an Academy Award, believe me. My grandma even says that I should be a bit more like Soledad, so sweet and clean. Yeah, clean, that is what grandma said, because grandma has a bit of OCD and likes everything shining like new. Even your fingernails.

But back to my friend. Soledad is the only one who knows EVERYTHING about me—like, that I have three dreams in life:

a) to live in Hawaii

b) to be openly gay, and

c) to marry a beautiful woman who knows how to surf and cook coconut shrimp.

But these are just that, dreams. Dreams that will most likely never become true because:

a) I haven't been to Hawaii since I left when I was a little girl and my grandparents refuse to go back or let me go

b) to be openly gay will mean breaking my grandparents' hearts and destroying their dream of me marrying a good man, and

c) how am I gonna marry a woman who surfs and cooks if I will probably end up marrying some stupid dude that my grandparents approve of?

Soledad keeps telling me I should not be so dramatic and pessimistic. Although she knows my grandparents pretty well, she really doesn't know what it means not only to live with them, but also to be the most important person in their lives.

It's beautiful, to be that, but it's also a burden. I feel like I can't fail them; I can never fail them.

JANUARY 19TH

Are you still there? Did I overwhelm you with so much information in just a few pages? I'm sorry, I can't help it, I talk a lot when I'm nervous and I guess writing my first diary is making me nervous.

I hope you're still on the other side of the page reading this and looking forward to reading more about me and my life. I'm still very young and haven't experienced all that much, but I have a freaking motherfucker imagination. You wouldn't believe all my mind has to share. I know, you are probably thinking I'm a walking contradiction: first I tell you I used to hate diaries, then I tell you I was convinced to start writing one, and now I can't stop writing in it. I can't help it, I have always been like this.

I guess you can say that's the cinematographic part of me. Oh, I didn't include this in my dreams list, but you must know that when I grow up, I wanna write/direct/produce films. I wanna be like Sofia Coppola (without the famous father, of course). I wanna write, direct, and produce my own movies. I love the movies. I love how a movie can let you escape from your reality and enter a new one.

I guess writing this diary is a bit like escaping from one reality and entering into the one you really want.

CHAPTER TWO
no lesbian skills

FEBRUARY 1ST

Today I heard some girls at school talking shit about Soledad and how crazy she is. They were obviously criticizing her for being so open about her life. Translation: they were criticizing her for being bisexual. I didn't dare say or do shit. These girls, they are all seniors, a group of skinny, raging blondes, the kind that you don't want to mess with. So even though I was so mad, I kept my mouth shut.

But I felt like yelling at them, at everybody. Have you ever felt like shouting something to the world, something deep and secret about you? Well,

I have. More and more, lately. I feel that urge all the freaking time. Today when I heard those girls talking shit about my friend, I felt like screaming. I wanted to yell, "SHE IS BI, SO WHAT? I AM A LESBIAN AND THAT'S NONE OF YOUR FUCKING BUSINESS."

But I didn't.

Part of me knows that if I had, gossip about me would have started. And sooner or later, word would get to my grandparents. If I had said something, I probably wouldn't have felt better anyway. No one would have started clapping or congratulating me for coming out in such a loud way. Really, no one would have cared, except maybe Soledad. She might have gone a little crazy and who knows, maybe she would have started stripping or something, singing songs about us being queer.

What stopped me? My fucking little voice. No, I'm not crazy, we all have a fucking little voice in the back of our heads, a voice that is always talking to us and preventing us from doing stupid shit.

Although, sometimes the little voice is the one that pushes us to do stupid shit. (I remember when my fucking little voice convinced me to shave my legs and I ended up cutting myself, not to mention Grandma almost killed me with her bare hands.) (She says good girls are not supposed to shave their legs and armpits before they turn eighteen. Can you imagine? Think of it, we girls start developing hair everywhere around thirteen, so five years of hair is like, too much, right?)

Most of the time this little voice helps me out. It's the one that says, "No, Mikala, don't do that," or, "Mikala, stop it, you are just gonna worry your grandparents." This voice works like the brakes on a car; it prevents you from crashing your existence.

So, no I did not yell at those stupid blonde girls.

I must tell you something: I have yelled, and I have publicly come out. It happened once in NYC, I got the balls to yell, "I LIKE GIRLS!"

Soledad laughed her ass at me, and then she added, "I LIKE GIRLS AND BOYS!"

There was a bunch of people around, people who stopped for like half a second to look at the crazy girls who had just yelled, and then they all continued with their lives. But then, from behind a trashcan, an old homeless man yelled, "I did too and look where I ended up." Soledad pulled my arm and we ran from the place.

Once in NYC, I also yelled, "I AM MIKALA AND I WANNA BE FREE."

The only thing I got was this old lady saying, "Oh, these Japanese people, they are so crazy." (If I had a dime for every time people confuse me for a Japanese, Chinese, Vietnamese, or Korean, I'd be rich. I wonder if a Japanese or a Korean person has ever been confused for a Hawaiian.)

Why did I do it? That's a very good question, Reader. I did it because I feel trapped. I did it for the same reason I started writing this diary, to get the burden of words, identity, and reality off my shoulders at least for a minute. And it felt good.

Yeah, sometimes I feel trapped. I'm sure you have too, at least once in your life.

I wish I had the balls to come out, to admit that I am a lesbian. Of course, I am a lesbian with no lesbian skills, but well, experience comes with time, doesn't it? I know I'm not ready, to come out, I mean. I am more than ready to practice some lesbian skills.

I am such a loser. I have never had sex, and the only time I made out with a girl was with Soledad and that doesn't count because we're friends and we were both drunk.

Yes, I made out with Soledad (no judgment, please). It was a mistake. It was something neither of us will ever do again, believe me. OK, I will be honest, it was more than making out. We got off. We didn't do anything to each other. Each one did herself. I don't think that counts as sex. Does it?

It all started with a kiss.

Wait, no. It started with me staying at her place when her parents were out at a party. It continued with her making me fix a couple of Mai Tais (with Grandpa's recipe, of course). The next thing I know we're tongue kissing—laughing—but tongue kissing. Touching here and there. Flashing boobs at each other (laughing at each other's boobs size; hers are almost flat, mine round and generous). Covering ourselves with a blanket on the sofa of her TV room and fingering, fingering, yes fingering ourselves while watching some semi-porn shit we got on the web.

Seriously, you must agree that masturbating next to your best friend who happens to be touching herself too can't count as sex.

Truth is we almost jeopardized our friendship for that. We had an endless dialogue that time.

Dialogue between Soledad and Mikala about Making Out

Me: You kissed me first.

Soledad: No, you did.

Me: I tell you, you did.

Soledad: No, no, no, *you* did.

Me: And then it was your idea to watch that video.

Soledad: Correction, it was my idea to watch *a* video. It was yours to watch precisely that one.

Me: But it was your idea to have *finger time*.

Soledad: It was you who came up with the concept of *finger time*.

Et cetera, et cetera, et cetera . . .

Confession time: this *event* used to be in my mind once in a while, back in the B.S. era, making out with a girl, having sex with a girl, hell, having a *relationship* with a girl. It was just a thought that flew by my mind like butterflies in spring. You see them, and then you don't see them.

But now, all I think about is girls, being with a girl. Finding *the* girl.

Reader, are you in love? Have you ever been in love? Is it as beautiful and painful as they say it is? I bet you know, I bet you have lost your mind once or twice because of a girl or a boy. Not me. I'm still waiting to lose my mind over *my* girl.

F EBRUARY 2ND NIGHT
Note to self: write a short story about two girls who live in a wonderful apartment in a wonderful city.

Note to self 2: the girls are in love, of course.

F EBRUARY 14TH
Letter from Mikala to Valentine's Day

Dear Valentine's Day,

Someone has to finally say it, someone has to open up to you, Valentine's Day. Be brave 'cause what you are about to hear might be hard to bear. The truth is, I hate you and I'm not the only one who does. You're just too much. So why don't you just go and fuck yourself, and when you're done, then please, just please find a wonderful girl for me.

With Hate,

Mikala Kekoa

FEBRUARY 17TH

Do you know who Ellen Page is? She's that cute actress, the one from that movie, *Juno,* and *Inception*. Yes, that little one, who looks like ten even though she is twenty-something. Anyway, Ellen Page is my hero. A few days ago, she was at this LGBT convention or something in Las Vegas and she came out, just like that. She said, "I'm here today because I am gay, and because maybe I can make a difference."

That girl has balls, right? You know what she's been telling the media? That she was, and I quote, "Tired of lying by omission." She came out to her parents when she was nineteen, but as time went by she kept thinking about it and she realized how she wanted, and I quote again, "To love someone freely and walk down the street and hold my girlfriend's hand."

Reader, let's clap together for Page's honesty. Fucking awesome.

Soledad doesn't like her; she says she's not really

her type. But Soledad changes her type every time she can. Just last week she said she had a thing for gingers, and yesterday she said that all red-haired girls are fake.

Soledad is kind of coming out little by little. Her balls are almost as big as Ellen Page's. When her mother asks her questions, like, if there's any boy in her life, Soledad says, "No, and there isn't any girl either." Her mother simply nods and smiles, as if Soledad was just messing around. I think Sole does it just to disrupt the normality in her family. Sometimes I believe she calls herself queer just to be the center of attention. See, she doesn't even see herself as lesbian, she says she likes both girls and boys. This makes her a bisexual and you know what they say about bisexuals. (In case you didn't know, everybody thinks that bisexuals are just confused people.) (I disagree.)

F EBRUARY 19TH
I was reading in Wikipedia about Hawaii
last night. (I know what people think about
Wikipedia, but believe me, I have found some
interesting stuff there.) By the way, did you know
that *wiki* means *quick* in Hawaiian? Interesting,
eh? Anyway, I read that, according to journal
entries by Captain Cook's crew (I need to find
out more about him), it was widely believed
that many Hawaiian warriors engaged in *aikāne*
relationships. (*Aikāne*= same sex relationships, I
told you this, remember?) The saying was, "If
you don't sleep with a man, how could you trust
him with your life when you go into battle?" It
makes sense; no one would protect you as much
as someone who really loves you.

I need a person to love me. I need a person to
love.

I need *aikāne*.

I should yell it at the ferry, "I NEED *AIKĀNE!*"

But who knows, people might think that *aikāne* is just a new drink or a new drug.

It's a beautiful word, isn't it? Repeat it after me: *aikāne, aikāne, aikāne, aikāne, aikāne, aikāne, aikāne, aikāne.*

February 20TH
Title: ASPEN LOVE

ACT I

BLACK.
We hear an alarm.

INTERIOR OF MIKALA'S BEDROOM.

Close-up on the brilliant colors of an Ikea rug, then the center of a king bed with bright pink covers. We slowly tilt up to discover the back of Mikala. She is naked and sleeping deeply. She finally notices the alarm clock ringing. Without opening her eyes she slowly reaches for it

*and turns it off. Her breath is calm and measured . . .
in and out . . . in and out.*

*Mikala (groaning): Oh, I am so tired; I could stay in
bed all day.*

*Mikala takes her time sitting down on her bed, her big
wonderful round tits in the air. She stretches, scratches
her pink hair. She then looks at the clock and notices
it's eleven a.m. She jumps from the bed. Close-up on a
photo next to the alarm. The photo shows Mikala and
Germaine, both of them are wearing traditional and
colorful Hawaiian skirts, and are holding piña coladas
in their hands.*

*Mikala: Germaine is probably done by now, damn, she
is gonna be mad.*

*Mikala runs around in circles in her bedroom. She opens
the window next to her bed, light comes in and we see
a beautiful balcony surrounded by snow. She goes to her
dresser, opens and closes the drawers and heads to the*

closet. Camera follows Mikala while we see the large space of her bedroom and the fancy furniture. She goes into a walk-in closet with lines and lines of shoes. Clothes are hung by color, it looks like a rainbow. The phone rings. Mikala runs around the room looking for it.

Mikala: Geez, where's my phone?

Close-up to Mikala's phone under the bed, next to a pink rubber vibrator. Her iPhone screen shows an incoming call from Germaine, the same picture of both of them in Hawaii blinks. Mikala follows the sound of her phone and finds it under the bed; she sees the vibrator and puts it on the bed. She answers.

Mikala: Hey, babe?
Germaine (jokingly): Let me guess, you stayed in bed 'til now.
Mikala (faking a serious tone): No, of course not, I was taking, doing, I was, oh baby, you're gonna get mad.
Germaine (interrupting): Don't tell me, you were running

around naked looking for your phone because you just woke up.

Mikala (laughing): Do you have a camera on me or what?

Germaine: Well, I hope you rested after all we did last night. I don't know about you, but my body aches everywhere.

Mikala (flirting): Everywhere? Do you need a massage?

Germaine: I sure do. Hey, you coming? I was thinking we should . . .

(Voice off screen, calling): Mikala.

Mikala: We should what?

Germaine: We should have lunch at Gino's. We haven't been there in a while.

(Voice off screen): Mikalaaaa, lunch is ready.

Mikala: Mmm, Gino's . . . Mozzarella calzone, my love.

(Voice off screen): Mikala, this is gonna get cold, come down.

Germaine: Sometimes I think you love mozzarella more than you love me.

Mikala: Of course not, I love mozzarella as much as I love you.

(Voice off screen): Mikala, if you don't come down this second your grandpa and I are going to eat your food.

Gotta wrap this up. Grandma is calling.

I wonder if Sofia Coppola's grandparents or parents also interrupted her when she was working on one of her scripts. Maybe this is why all the really famous screenwriters are men, because their families did not take women seriously.

Grandma: Mikala, I am eating your rice now.

Me: I'm coming, I'm coming.

I am sorry, Reader, duty calls. For my grandparents, it is very important that we eat together. They think that sharing a meal is a way to share love.

I will come back later. Please, read again the beginning of my script and tell me what you think. I need feedback. How am I going to become the most famous lesbian screenwriter and director if I don't know if what I'm doing is any good?

F EBRUARY 25TH NIGHT
Today I was watching *The Hunger Games*, the *Catching Fire* one. I first saw it in the theater with Soledad. She read the books. I haven't. I should. Anyway, I was bored, so I made myself some popcorn and sat down to watch it again at home. Soledad says I only watch it because of Johanna Mason (played by hot Jena Malone). She's right, but Johanna isn't the only one I melt for. I also like Katniss (in a very *Oh, she is such a brave girl* kinda way).

Anyway, I watched the movie only to come to the conclusion that even though I like the romantic tension, triangle, or whatever between Katniss, Peeta, and Gale, I think the story is missing a great opportunity. Katniss should be with Johanna. Yes, sir. Think about it, it so makes sense. Like today, as I was watching that scene when Johanna strips naked in the elevator in front of Haymitch, Katniss, and Peeta, I had an epiphany: Johanna is not stripping to shock the guys, she is doing it to seduce Katniss. She is a lesbian.

The problem is that I didn't keep the thought for myself, I yelled. (My inner voice did not fucking stop me.) Grandma heard me. I tried to be a bit brave, but let's say things didn't end up that well.

Me: Man, Johanna and Katniss belong together. Why can't anyone see that?

Grandma: What do you mean?

Me: Nothing, nothing. Just something about this movie.

Grandma: What movie?

Me: *The Hunger Games*, Grandma, really it's nothing. Sorry if I was too loud.

Grandma: Oh, that's the second one? I like that better than the first one, you know that. I like how all of them create an alliance. (Yeah, my grandma likes *The Hunger Games*. Can you believe that?)

Me: Yes.

(I was hoping the conversation would end there.)

Grandma: But what were you saying about

Katniss and Johanna, Johanna is the grumpy one, right?

Me: Yes, that's Johanna, the grumpy-sexy one that everyone hates.

Grandma: But what about her and Katniss, what did you say?

I just sat there, not saying anything. Trying not to blush.

Grandma: Mikala?

Me: I said that . . . I said that Katniss and Johanna belong together.

Grandma: Oh . . . you mean, like a pair of lesbians?

If I had balls, this conversation could have gone like this:

Me: Yes, grandma, like a pair of lesbians.

Grandma: Oh, I don't know.

Me: You don't know what, Grandma?

Grandma: I don't know how I feel about lesbians.

Me: Well, Grandma, you better make up your mind about them lesbians.

Grandma: Me, why?

Me: Because I have news Grandma, I am a lesbian. Yes, Grandma, your only granddaughter is a fair member of the LGBT community. I am a lesbian, yes, Grandma, I am and I am proud of it.

Grandma: (look of shock on her face)

But of course, I don't have the balls (not even the metaphorical ones), and I didn't say any of this, although, check this out, I did try after I paused the movie:

Me: I said that . . . I said that Katniss and Johanna belong together.

Grandma: Oh . . . you mean, like a pair of lesbians?

Me: Yes, what, ahem, do you think? I mean, at the end it's Johanna who saves Katniss, remember?

Grandma: Well, yes, but . . .

Me: Grandma, do you dislike gay people? I mean, like, gay relationships?

Grandma: No, not at all. I have always been quite polite with Cecilia and Teresa, the Mexican girls from the flower shop. They are a couple, you know?

Me: Yes, but . . .

Grandma: So no, I am not against that. Of course not. We have told you about the *Māhū*, your grandfather and I, so we understand that there are different kinds of relationships.

Me: But . . .

Grandma: But I think that happens after you've been through everything in your life.

Me: You mean, if nothing else works.

Grandma: What I'm saying is that young people don't know as much. They can be confused. Where you see love between Johanna and Katniss, I see friendship.

Me: But . . .

Grandma: Imagine if people thought that you and Soledad were girlfriends, when you are only best friends.

Me: Yeah.

Grandma: By the way, talking about friendship

and love, did I tell you Ikaika called today? He was looking for you.

Me: No.

Dear Reader, I haven't told you about Ikaika. I haven't fully told you about my grandparents' obsession with getting me a boyfriend. They want me and Ikaika to be together, even though Ikaika and I have seen each other like only two times.

Anyway, my epiphany about Johanna and Katniss became a long conversation with Grandma about Ikaika and how much she likes him and how much she believes I should date him. It didn't matter that I told her that I cannot date someone who hasn't asked me to. Grandma says that sometimes girls can take the initiative.

Grandma: I was the one who asked your Grandpa to dance, and after a week or so, we were a couple. We got married less than a year after that.

I have heard the story a million times, and although I find it fascinating (even perfect material for a movie), this time I wasn't up for it. I ended up turning off my movie and here I am, back in my room, and back in my closet.

Oh, Reader. I wish I were you. You can skip all the pages you want and read the end of this diary, and know what my life turned into. You know my future, and I, well, I know shit. I better go to sleep. Who knows, maybe I can be in a love triangle with Johanna and Katniss in my dreams. Maybe I can finally practice my lesbian skills with them (let's hope Grandma or Ikaika don't interfere). (Shit, why did I say that? Now I just jinxed my lesbian dream.)

CHAPTER THREE
radiating queerness

MARCH 8TH

Grandma sent me to the flower shop. She loves having fresh flowers at home every week. I guess it's part of her Hawaiian blues. She likes all flowers, but give her yellow flowers—any type of yellow flowers—and you make her happy. Anyway, I went to the flower shop in our neighborhood. The Lesbian Flower Shop. (OK, that's not the name of the store, but it should be.) It's run by Cecilia and Teresa, who are a couple.

I like to see them. I like to hear them talk to each other. I like how they smile, joke, at many things. I also like it when they argue, because it doesn't feel like an argument. I wish I were friends with them, that way I could know more about the queer world.

When they just opened the shop everybody believed they were sisters, but it took one big French kiss in the middle of the neighborhood park to clear things up.

Cecilia is the older one, she is like forty or something. She is tall and skinny and has tattoos on both her arms. Teresa has an amazing body. You should see her butt, very Jennifer Lopez. (Is Jennifer Lopez Mexican?) Her thing is piercings, she has them everywhere. Well, I don't actually know if they're *everywhere*, but she does have a lot on her face: eyebrows, ears, nose, lips.

I admire them, you know? They live together, they own their shop, they bike everywhere, and they have a dog. They have everything they need to be happy. And they own their identity. They don't give a fuck who knows it. I want something like that when I grow up (a girl, not a shop). I see myself in Hawaii, surfing, biking, hiking with a wonderful woman next to me. Both of us radiating queerness and happiness and love. So much love.

MARCH 9TH

Oh, Reader, these past days have been a nightmare. I wanna tell you all about it, but I am so tired. Just came back from a date. Yes, a date. But not the kind of date I wish I had. No, no, no.

I went on a date with Ikaika. Yes, it was a little surprise from my grandma. And well, I have no words to describe it. I need to take a shower to rinse all this off, and then go to bed. I promise I will write all about it tomorrow.

MARCH 10TH

So I took a shower, put on my PJs and went to bed. I closed my eyes and started thinking. I basically had to force myself to sleep—only I couldn't sleep. When I opened my eyes to look at the clock, I saw that it was midnight and I closed them again. Started counting sheep. One, two, three, four, five . . . between sheep numbers one hundred twenty-three and one hundred twenty-four, I opened my eyes again. It was one fifteen a.m. and I still could not sleep. So I decided to come back to my diary and tell you about what happened earlier tonight.

The best way to do it is through fiction, just like we do in my Creative Writing class. Here we go.

Boy Meets Girl
by Mikala Kekoa

This is not the first time the boy and girl see each other, but it's the first time they go out. Her name is Mia. His is Ike. "If you don't like dating, let's imagine this is not dating," he told her to obviously calm her down. She smiled, but it was clear she was still nervous.

What Mia didn't tell Ike is that she did like dating,

she just didn't want to date men. Yes, Mia, beautiful Mia, sexy Mia, was lesbian.

They had dinner at her favorite pizza place. "Well, I might not date men, but I do like pizza," she thought when he suggested the place. After ordering a pepperoni and bacon with extra cheese, and an order of BBQ wings, he held her hand and said, "I need to talk to you about something." She thought, "You can talk to me about anything, but give me back my hand." As if he could hear her thoughts, he let go of her hand. She took a sip of her ~~Dr. Pepper Cherry-Cola wine~~ beer. He then said, "~~Darling sweetie~~ Mia . . . I am gay."

Mia spat her ~~Dr. Pepper Cherry-Cola wine~~ beer in Ike's face and said, "You're WHAT?"

M ARCH 11ᵀᴴ

So, yes, big surprise. Ikaika is gay. He's even been dating a guy for almost a year now. And no one knows. Obviously the guy knows, and now I know too. It really caught me off guard. We were having pizza and drinking soda, talking about school and weather, you know, the kind of things you talk about with people you don't really know. Then he told me, he knew I was uncomfortable and that he understood that. He knew that my grandparents and his parents had arranged our "date." I nodded. Then it came—an awkward silence, the longest ever. Ikaika looked at me and asked if he could be honest with me. I said yes. He asked then if I could keep a secret. (That got me interested, I must say, I guess it was only then that I started paying attention to him.)

Ikaika: Believe me, Mikala, I like you and everything, and I'm sure that if you got to know me better you would like me too.

Me: Okay.

Ikaika: The thing is, if I accepted this, you know, going out with you, it was because . . .

Me: Let me help you, it was *because* your parents, like my grandparents, want to decide everything in your life, right?

Ikala: Well, yes. Kinda.

Me: Look Ikaika, you don't have to explain *anything* to me. Really, it's fine. You don't have to *court* me or anything. Let's just eat our pizza, then we can part ways, and no hard feelings. *Believe* me . . .

Ikaika: No, the thing is. I do wanna date you.

(And this is when, dear Reader, I spit all my Dr. Pepper on Ikaika's face. This is one of these moments where reality meets fiction.)

Me: You wanna what? WHY? You don't even know me!

Ikaika: No, I don't wanna date you, I mean I do, but not like that. Damn it, it was all so clear in my mind earlier today. You know, what I wanted to tell you.

Me: OK, so now I'm confused, you wanna date me or not? Either way, I'm not interested. The truth is I came for the pizza and the wings, buddy.

Ikaika: You are one funny girl, I tell you. OK, let me try this again. Mikala, can I be honest with you? Can I share a secret with you?

Me: Yes, Ikaika, you can. Didn't we do this part already?

Ikaika: I am gay. I am gay and my parents would kill me if they found out. Maybe not my mom, but my dad would. He's on my back all the time. And then he mentioned you, and how your grandparents were looking for someone for you.

Me: Wait, what? My grandparents what? That is not how they sold this whole thing to me, they told me . . . Wait, it doesn't matter, continue please, I'm intrigued.

Ikaika: Well, when they told me about you, I thought I should just do it, I should just go ahead and do what my dad wanted me to. Dating you could mean him letting me be. He would relax and I could continue with my life with Tom-Tom for now.

Me: Tom-Tom?

Ikaika: Yes, my boyfriend. You'll like him. I thought that if you do decide to date me, we could go out, the three of us once in a while.

Me: Are you out of your mind? What makes you think that I would agree to something like that?

Ikaika: Because you seem cool.

Me: I seem cool?

Ikaika: Yes, and . . .

Me: And?

Ikaika: And your friend Soledad told me you're gay. She said you need me as much as I need you.

Me: speechless

Ikaika: Look, the pizza is here.

Me: speechless again

Long story short, Soledad and Tom-Tom, Ikaika's boyfriend, know each other. They talked, and somehow Ikaika, me, and the matchmaking came into the conversation and they ended up planning this. I know this whole thing sounds incredible and unbelievable, Reader, but I swear it is all truth.

Ikaika and I ended up talking a lot. He told me his story, which is kinda sad, really. His dad sounds like a macho guy who's been forcing Ikaika to be what he's not. He has even been violent with him (I was curious about *how* violent, but I didn't dare to ask what he meant).

I totally understand how Ikaika sees "dating" me as a way out. His story moved me so much that I agreed to go along with this lie. But then, he went nuts.

Ikaika: Thank you, thank you Mikala. This will work great, we will help each other.

Me: Don't say thank you, just know that you are gonna pay for the pizza now and forever.

Ikaika: You know, if this works out, we can help each other for life. You know, we can even get married. I bet my mother could help us find and pay the rent for an apartment in NY. We can all live there together, you, Tom-Tom, me, maybe your girlfriend.

Me: Wait, wait, hold your horses. Look: a) I don't have a girlfriend, b) If I did I would not take her to live in a commune, and c) I will not marry you. Are you fucking out of your mind? We-can't-get-married.

Ikaika: Why not? This would solve everything for us, there would be no need to come out to our families. Imagine our wedding invitations:

Mr. and Mrs. Kekoa and Mr. and Mrs. Smith request the honor of your presence at the marriage of Mikala and Ikaika

Ikaika: See, our names look wonderful together even on a napkin. Now imagine them on a nice piece of paper.

Me: Shut up, give me that. Jesus, no Ikaika, we can't get married, we can't. It's a lie. I don't know about you, but I already feel like I'm living a lie, and I don't plan to live forever in a lie.

Ikaika: I guess you're right.

Me: Of course I am.

Ikaika: So.

Me: So?

Ikaika: Are we not dating then?

I ended up accepting, again. I did it for him, yes, but I also did it for me. No, not only for me, I did it for my grandparents. I know it will make them very happy to see that I am dating someone they approve of. Unlike Luana, who would date goats if she could. It was funny because once the conversation with Ikaika changed direction, I could see him as he is, radiating queerness when talking about his boyfriend.

So, yes. I have officially started dating. High five, Reader! (Just kidding.)

MARCH 13TH
Ikaika invited me to the movies tonight. He says we have to hang out together. I told him that we could *say* we were going to the movies and then each of us could go anywhere and do something on our own. He said no, he says he actually wants to hang out with me; I am pretty much his first lesbian

friend. I guess that makes him my first gay friend. He wants us to really get to know each other. "Maybe some other time we can do that, or we can all hang out together, you know Soledad, Tom-Tom, you, and me." Translation: he is cool, he wants us to be friends. Wait, does he think Soledad is my lesbian girlfriend?

March 13th Night

So, we didn't go to the movies. We ended up stuffing ourselves with sushi and mochi ice cream. We talked for hours. I like Ikaika, I think we really hit it off. When Ikaika dropped me off, I texted Soledad to tell her all about my "date," but she pretty much ignored me. She just vented about her mother. They had yet another argument. (Soledad and her mom argue all the freaking time, most of the time about stupid stuff.) I tried to distract her by telling her how Ikaika suggested we should "double-date" with him and Tom-Tom, but she said, "Yeah, whatever, now let's get back to my favorite subject: ME."

My friend can be real bitchy sometimes. (Did I say bitchy? OMG, I mean selfish, selfish.)

Note to self: Schedule that double date soon.

March 15th

Soledad's cousin lives in NY; she is a law student. Her roommates happen to be going to Florida for spring break. So, she will have the apartment to herself and she has invited Soledad to visit, and Soledad has invited me.

Dialogue between Soledad and Mikala about Going to NY:

Soledad: Mika, my cousin, she is awesome. She shares a huge apartment with some girls but they will all be away on vacation. My cousin can't go because she has an internship and . . . Anyway, get this, she invited me to go and hang out there for spring break.

Me: Oh, that's cool. I mean, not the part where she'll be working.

Soledad: You should totally come with me.

Me: Oh, that'd be fantastic, but I don't think my grandparents will allow it.

Soledad: You think?

Me: No chance. They worry too much. Besides, Ikaika said we could do something fun, all of us.

Soledad: Ikaika, Ikaika . . . Bitch, are you falling in love with him?

Me: Ugh, no, that'd be disgusting. I just like hanging out with him.

Soledad: Come on, let's go to NY. It's not like we'll be on our own. A grown-up will be with us. I bet your grandparents will let you go once they know my cousin is a lawyer.

Me: I dunno, Sole. You know how strict they can be sometimes.

Soledad: What if you make Ikaika ask permission. He could even come along, him and Tom-Tom.

Me: Ha, in your dreams. My grandparents would never accept that.

Soledad: Come on, bitch, give it a try. Didn't you guys say that you wanted the four of us to hang out and double date? This is our chance.

Soledad had a point. NYC. The four of us. Spring break. Why not?

MARCH 15TH NIGHT
Mikala's Phrases of the Week:

- *Pussies are hard work.*
- *My sex life and me are boring, not bored.*
- *I like women who smile as if they had just seen a panda eating bamboo.*

CHAPTER FOUR
scoring

MARCH 20TH

Spring break. Is. Almost. Here. Insert. A. Happy. Face. Few more days and we are all free.

(Don't worry, Reader, you will have all the details of our trip. You know you are part of the gang.)

NYC. Here. We. Go.

MARCH 23RD

Ikaika and Tom-Tom are picking us up. The four of us, Soledad, Ikaika, Tom-Tom, and me, are having dinner together to plan our trip. We are having a fabulous spring break in Manhattan. Yes, my grandparents agreed. Of course, there had to be some lying here and there so we could all go. Let me explain.

Lie #1: Soledad told her parents that she and I have this art project, and we need to visit the MoMA and the Guggenheim in NYC. She has told them that my boyfriend is coming along to take care of us and that obviously their niece will make sure that we all behave.

Lie #2: We are telling the same lie to my grandparents, only we are highlighting the fact that her cousin will be there as our chaperone.

Lie #3: Ikaika is telling his parents he's going for the whole week to take care of his girlfriend and her BFF. And that there are separate bedrooms for girls and guys. (Which will probably be true.)

As you can see, Tom-Tom is not included in any of the scenarios. Fortunately, he is the only one who actually doesn't have to lie. His parents, as it seems, are quite cool with the fact that,

a) Their son is gay, and

b) he is going to NYC for a week with

c) his boyfriend and two more friends.

Tom-Tom's life is way better than ours.

We still don't know exactly what we will do, but one thing is clear, there will be no supervision for a week. Woohoo!

Gotta go. Soledad is reading all this and I hate it when she does that. Plus the boys will be here any minute now.

March 25th

We just got to NY. The apartment is teeny-tiny, but still pretty awesome for a graduate student. Soledad and I left the bedroom for Tom-Tom and Ikaika. It's only fair since they are paying for most of the trip. Let's say this is their honeymoon with two hairy dykes included. (If Soledad reads this she will get so mad, maybe that will teach her not to read *my* stuff.) We just dropped our things off, and we'll be heading to the MoMA in a bit. We lied about the art project, but we didn't lie about going to museums. We are kinda nerds, Soledad and me.

The guys will stay at the apartment. They are meeting us later to go to the Empire State Building.

MARCH 26TH

I called my grandparents early today because it's Prince Kuhio's Day. This day is very important for Hawaiians. I really don't know much about it; I just know that at home we always celebrate it as if it was July 4th (just no fireworks). When I was little we would have a party with their best friends, Mr. and Mrs. Jujio (who by the way are spring breaking in Hawaii—it's like everyone is in Hawaii but me). My grandparents asked me how things were going in the city. It's the first time they let me travel on my own. The next time I travel on my own, it will be to Hawaii (but the way I see it, they would only let me go if I were married to Ikaika).

Only Soledad and I are up. Tom-Tom and Ikaika went to a gay club last night. The doorman drew huge Xs on the back of their hands, so they would be identified as minors and no alcohol would be sold to them. But it seems that DID NOT stop them from getting drinks here and there from some guys they met. So now, they are hung over and us girls are making them breakfast before we hit the city (actually, Soledad is making them a *tortilla española*, which really is a potato omelet if you ask me).

Today we are going to the Guggenheim, then we'll have lunch at Central Park. Tom-Tom says we must walk all over Fifth Avenue 'til we lose our feet. Soledad wants to go to the club the guys went to last night. We had a bit of an argument about it.

Soledad: Come on, say yes, Mika. This might be our chance to score.

Me: Scoring, me? I'm too slow for that.

Soledad: Well, see it as practice, Mika.

Me: Stop with the Mika calling, you know I don't like it.

Soledad: Mika, I will stop calling you Mika, if you say yes. Yes? Yes?

Me: Fine, we'll go to that club.

Soledad: I don't know why you play hard to get. You know you wanna go anyways. It's not like you're doing it for me.

Dear Reader, it's not like I was playing hard to get. It's just that this seems like a big deal. This will be my first time in an actual gay bar, with actual lesbians. It kinda makes me nervous.

MARCH 27TH

Reader, it's three a.m. Everyone is asleep around here. Everyone but me. Tonight was way better than I expected. I am serious, I felt like I was in an episode of that old show, *The L World*, only the NYC-Teen version.

NYC has the best lesbians in the world (not that I have a lot of material to compare it with, though, except for Soledad).

We ended up hanging out with these girls who happen to be from NJ, and are staying with a friend in Greenwich. Their names are Gina and Tracy.

They're juniors like us. We hit it off. It wasn't clear to us if they were a couple or if they were just BFFs like Soledad and me, but we had an amazing time together.

It seems like Gina and Tracy are also kind of new at this thing called being *queer*. It was nice to see that we're not the only ones in the world who don't know what the fuck they are doing when it comes to *queer* life.

I should be sleeping, but I can't. This is the first time that I feel like myself. The first time I get to talk about girls with girls. The first time I get to discuss Katniss's boobs or Taylor's Swift too-skinny ass.

The first time I feel part of something—as myself, not a fake version of myself.

We are meeting them later today for lunch. We exchanged phone numbers and emails, and decided to hang out with them.

OK. Sleepy now. Gotta go.

March 28ᵀᴴ

So, I wanna tell you about today. But the best way to do it is in the present tense. Imagine you are with us. Reader, you paying attention? OK. Here we go:

We are at Central Park, again. You see us? I am the one with the I LOVE ME t-shirt (pretty badass, right?) and Soledad is sitting next to me. Don't you love her flowery skirt? We are with the two girls we met last night. Gina is the brunette and Tracy is the blond one. Yes, both of them are very tall. Now, do you recognize where we are? Yup, we are sitting near the Alice in Wonderland statue. As you can see we are all talking and talking. You, Reader, you are listening.

Gina: So, how did you like the bar last night?

Soledad: It was great. That DJ, he's *out of this world*, right?

Tracy: What do you mean? Are you being rude?

Soledad: What? No, I'm not criticizing him. His mixes were excellent.

Gina: Tracy, Tracy, wait, I don't think she's insinuating anything else. Right, Soledad?

Soledad: Insinuating what? Dude, I'm lost. What the fuck are you talking about?

Tracy: Geez, girl. The DJ, Harry, is transitioning.

Me: Transitioning? Oh, you mean, like, he used to be a she?

Gina: Yes, and Miss LGBT Politics here thought your friend meant, you know, something else.

Soledad: No, not at all. I am a bitch but not *that* bitch.

Me: Wow, you can't even tell. He just seemed like a gay dude to me. And you, sweet friend, you *are* a bitch all the time.

Soledad: Shut up, Mika. Wait so, now I'm interested, is he into chicks or into dudes? Cause I found him very, very handsome.

Gina and Tracy: Yes, he is.

Oh, Reader, it is then when it happened. It is then that my world rocked. *She* arrived. *She* came to us. *She*. I hadn't even seen her when I heard her voice, and still my world, I tell you, my world rocked. I get goose bumps just to think about it now.

She: Who is very handsome? Don't tell me you two became straight last night.

Gina and Tracy: Frieda, you made it!

Frieda: Yes, Dad finally gave me a break. He and his wife wanted to have some family time with me. We went to have sushi and they let me go.

If this was a movie, this scene would have been this way:

The off-camera voice that we first heard, becomes a body, a few seconds later it becomes a beautiful creature, as if the Alice in Wonderland statue had come to life. The camera scans the body of a beautiful blonde girl—the "she" Mikala has been waiting for her whole life.

Movie moment is over when the blonde girl continues talking as if she was a normal human being and not the most perfect girl.

Frieda: Anyway, tell me everything, how did

it go, where did you guys go? Hey, have we met before?

No, Reader, no. She was not talking to me. Beautiful Alice in Wonderland was not addressing me. She was talking to Soledad. Soledad, who is an exotic creature from paradise, and not a short kinda chubby Hawaiian girl. (In case you forgot, that is me.)

As you know, Soledad is an attention whore, so obviously she jumped up from her seat and introduced herself. "No, I don't think we've met before, at least not in this life. Hi, my name is Soledad." Gina and Tracy then introduced me and updated Frieda on who we *both* were, and how we met.

Gina: They're from NJ too and they're also having their spring break here, so we decided to include them in our *Wild on Manhattan*.

Frieda: Damn, and now I missed the first episode. Right? I missed a hell of a night, eh?

Tracy: You did. Plus, you missed an amazing fundraiser for HIV Teens.

Gina: Oh, Tracy, don't start with that; please don't pull out your agenda on us right now. Today is about having fun; today is about getting to know the LGBTNYC scene.

Soledad: Ha, it sounds like *lgbteeny*.

Frieda: It does, so what's the plan?

Me: To conquer the world, Pinky.

Go ahead Reader, laugh. Laugh all you want because that is what I said. Can you believe what a dork I can be? Good thing they all laughed, so at least I didn't feel *that* stupid after all. Frieda even said, "I've always said Pinky and Brain were a couple."

I added, "Just like Ernie and Bert from Sesame Street." We both laughed. I made eye contact, which in *queer* flirting means A LOT.

MARCH 28TH

We had a blast today. We hung out all afternoon with Gina, Tracy, and beautiful, gorgeous, wonderful, Frieda. I was kind of dorky, all shy and nervous when around Frieda. Soledad, as always, was so full of herself, all charming and funny. Tracy and Gina, well, they spent the rest of the day arguing and making up. (I said making up, not making out, but if you asked me, I think those two would do a lot better making out, there's this tension between them.)

Tomorrow the three of them are coming to our apartment; the plan is to get a bit wasted and then hit the club again. Soledad told them about my Mai Tai recipe. So, a wonderful night seems to be ahead of us. Yes, all five of us. Yes, I am the fifth wheel. Yes, yes. I can bet that alcohol and dancing will have everyone scoring but me.

MARCH 29TH MIDNIGHT

We had dinner first. I got to sit next to Frieda and I got to talk to her a lot. First she asked me what my name meant. Then, next thing I know we are talking as if we had known each other forever. She's so smart and awesome. We have so much in common. We have read almost the same stuff and we are both interested in the arts. She wants to be an off Broadway actress. I told her I was into writing, and she suggested I write a monologue for her to use for future auditions.

Soledad found our conversation too boring I guess because she kept herself apart (also, she was flirting with our waitress who had tattoos on both her arms).

Frieda kept talking to me. We realized we have similar tastes. Sofia Coppola's movies, Sara Blaedel's mystery novels, and music by Crystal Castles. I flirted. She flirted. Or maybe neither of us flirted, but something did happen. I can tell. The way she smiled at me once in a while, the way she touched my shoulder or my arm when she talked to me. It gives me chills just to think about it. Honestly, Reader, at some point I thought, *this is it*, this is the night when I get to kiss *the* girl.

After dinner we went to the club, the same place where we met. It was there that everything went to hell. The music and the party-mood at the place drove us apart. We danced. No, not Frieda and me, we *all* danced together. Sucks, right?

Group dancing made flirting impossible. I did my best to dance next to Frieda, to try and have her for myself, but it didn't work. When it comes to dancing, Soledad is the queen, so she got everyone's attention. Frieda was fascinated by my friend's sexy moves. It wasn't clear to me if Soledad, while dancing, was flirting with Frieda or with the DJ, the trans boy we were all talking about the other day. (Now that I think about it, knowing Soledad, she was probably dancing-flirting with both Frieda and the DJ at the same time. Who knows?)

I sat down with Tracy and Gina trying to gossip with all that noise. They were talking about Soledad. Gina's words, "So is she bisexual or what?"

Tracy laughed and then looked at me and asked, "Tell us."

I was straight. I told them sometimes I thought

she was a little bit of both, "But her balance goes more to the attention whore part." We laughed.

"You are the perfect combination of funny and honest," Tracy told me. I felt important.

Maybe I shouldn't have said that about my friend, but to tell you the truth I have always thought that. I mean, she claims to be bisexual, but really she is more like a bisexual in theory. It's like she'd say anything just to get everyone's attention. For example, after dancing, we all went to get hot dogs, and every time someone said something, Soledad interrupted by saying, "No wait, I have something better," or "Listen to this first." Competition, that's what drives Soledad.

MARCH 30TH EARLY IN THE MORNING
Everyone is sleeping now. I am the nerd who carried the diary in her bag and is writing now.

We are at Frieda's. She invited us to spend the night after the club. Her parents are divorced, so Frieda lives with her mom in NJ and comes and visits her dad here in the city every once in a while. It's a very nice apartment where everything seems brand new and expensive. He seems like a guy who says yes to everything his daughter asks.

MARCH 30TH AFTERNOON

Frieda's dad and his wife even left pancakes for all of us before going to work. We didn't eat them, we devoured them. Soledad kept us entertained; she got the DJ's number and email. Can you believe that? Gina dared her to call him and invite him for a coffee.

Frieda was just quietly drinking black coffee. (Seriously, who drinks coffee without sugar, cream, or milk?) She ignored us all. It was like she was a whole different person. I asked her, "Are you OK?"

And she simply nodded, smiled, and said, "I like watching people after a party. It's funny, isn't it?"

I said, "Yeah, like where did the glamour go?"

She laughed. I love that she laughs at the stupid shit I say.

"Hey, what is it that you do in that little notebook that you carry around?" Yes, Reader, she saw us: you, me, and the notebook.

I said, "Oh, I just like scribbling stuff once in a while."

But you and I, Reader, you and I, we know it's more than that.

So, everything was going well. We were all chatting and being silly and then, my phone started to ring. First I thought, "Shit, Grandma." I hadn't called her since the day before. But no, it wasn't her. It was Luana. I didn't reply. Minutes later, a second call, and then a text. Luana never texts unless she in trouble and needs her parents and/ or her daughter to help her out. That changed my mood. I went to the bathroom and when I got out Frieda was there.

"Everything OK?" she said.

"Yeah," I said. "It's just my, ehm, my mom." Frieda's smile disappeared.

She said, "Moms suck." I couldn't agree more.

We left around three p.m. Our new friends made us promise to keep in touch.

MARCH 30TH NIGHT
We are having an early dinner before heading back home. Everyone is in the kitchen cooking but me. Don't roll your eyes, Reader, I needed to update you.

Ikaika and Tom-Tom look like shit. Those two had a sex marathon I guess, because they look tired and weary. Soledad told them everything about last night, and about our new group of friends, and about the DJ.

Ikaika looked at me and whispered in my ear, "And my girlfriend, did she meet someone special?" I didn't answer, but I'm pretty sure my smile gave it away.

MARCH 30TH MIDNIGHT
Things Mikala Learned in NYC

- *She knows how to make people laugh.*
- *She needs to improve her dancing skills.*
- *She likes Frieda.*
- *She likes NY pizza and hot dogs.*
- *Men are noisy when they have sex.*

CHAPTER FIVE

A PRIL 2ND
  Title: HAWAIIAN FEVER

ACT I

BLACK.
We hear some drums playing slowly. A sexy tune.

EXTERIOR. MOUNTAINS, PALM TREES, AND THEN THE OCEAN.

Close-up of a female figure wearing a red and orange swimsuit. We slowly tilt up to discover the profile of

Mikala. She is staring at the ocean, a surfboard under her arm.

Mikala (Off Screen Voice): I can't believe I'm here. Finally here.

Mikala lets her surfboard fall on the sand. She sits next to it, then lays down on the sand. Camera examines her body. Both her ankles have colorful bracelets. Her legs, her knees. Her whole body is observed closely.

Frieda: Are you ready for adventure?

Mikala looks up and finds her lover smiling at her. She stands up and Frieda pulls her in for a long French kiss. Her arms on Mikala's shoulders. Mikala's hands on Frieda's perfect round butt.

Mikala: I could be like this forever.
(Off Screen Voice): What are you doing Mikala?
(Off Screen Voice): Mikala? Mikala, are you awake?

Sometimes I think Grandma lies low, waiting for me to start typing on my laptop to call me and interrupt my writing.

Me: Yes, Grandma, of course I'm awake. I'm writing, see?

Grandma: Sorry, sweetie, you seemed lost for a second. Hey, your mother's been calling. I didn't answer, but I'm starting to feel worried. Would you call her?

This is the thing: after all Luana has put my grandparents through, they just decided to cut her off. They don't look for her, they don't reply to her calls or emails. I am in charge of that. If she needs something from them, she asks me, and I ask them. When I say *something*, I mean money. Luana only calls when she needs money.

Me: If it's important she will call or text me again.

Grandma: I'm worried.

Me: Grandma, don't be. You know her. If she really can't solve this herself, she will call and call 'til we help her.

Grandma smiles at me, a fake smile that actually says, "Yeah, you are right." And yes, I know I'm right. I know Luana is my mother, and I know her better than anyone even though we haven't actually lived together. I know it wouldn't hurt to pick up the phone and get this over with, but we have a life, too.

You gotta understand. It's not easy. It is never easy with my mother. If I can be honest, I think calling her *mother* is giving her too much credit. I call her Luana, it was either that or calling her *the-woman-who-gave-birth-to-me*, which is too long.

On those rare occasions that I talk about her with people who don't really know her, I say Luana this or Luana that, and people go, "Luana, is she your sister?" I say no. "She's my mother, but she's not a normal mother."

You see, normal mothers know their daughters' favorite color, food, and cartoons. Normal mothers build a home for their daughters. Normal mothers who, for some legal reason, don't get to live with their daughters, try to see them every other week-end, or call them every other day, or send them long letters that smell like peaches, and once in a while give them a gift.

Do I need to tell you that Luana has never done ANY of these things?

Miss Moore says that crazy mothers and drunken fathers make great themes and wonderful characters for fiction. Mine would win an award for her performance because mine is not fiction and is actually both, crazy and drunk. (I'm so damn lucky, right?) *The-woman-who-gave-birth-to-me* is just too fucked up, and will never change.

There are moments when she isn't *that* bad. It doesn't happen often. But once every million years she goes through a phase in which she writes emails with poems or links to poems on the web. Once every million years, she visits without driving us all crazy. One Christmas she brought gifts for everybody and cooked for us, or maybe that's something I dreamt.

Most of the time, Luana is just Luana. The teen who didn't grow up. When she calls it's because she needs help, which always translates into money, which always translates into drama. If we had a penny for every time she fucked up we would be living in a penthouse in NYC and not in a townhouse in NJ.

In middle school my counselor told me that maybe my mother's behavior was a result of guilt, her own guilt at having abandoned me, her own guilt for making my grandparents suffer so much. Whatever.

April 3rd
A Brief Summary of Luana's Life

1. *Luana is an only child, the first born after a couple of miscarriages. Luana becomes Mr. and Mrs. Kekoa's little princess. She gets it all: dolls, pets, bikes, trips, surfing lessons, and expensive surfboards.*

2. *Luana started smoking pot somewhere between middle school and high school. I am sure many kids start more or less at that age, and more or*

less for the same reasons, peer pressure, and to show off. But I am sure not many kids started also dealing pot and got expelled for it.

3. Luana traded pot for cocaine. A more expensive "hobby" as you can imagine. Expensive "hobbies" require a higher income. First, she became a surfing instructor herself. Then, when that wasn't enough, she started stealing from her parents. Next, she stole from men she dated.

4. One of Luana's boyfriends, one with Luana's same "hobby" most likely, turned the night a little too violent. She ended up in the hospital. She learned her lesson.

5. Luana in Rehab.

6. Luana out of Rehab and back with her "hobby."

7. Luana gone, her parents would lose sight of her for days, weeks, and months. Detectives are not cheap.

8. Luana would come back looking like a stray cat who just got out of a fight. Hurt, depressed, lost. High.

9. Repeat points 4, 5 and 6 a couple more years, until . . .

10. *Luana comes back looking, again, like a stray cat. A pregnant stray cat. My grandparents made sure no alcohol, no drugs, no men, would be around Luana during her pregnancy. Their words, "This baby will change your life."*

11. *The baby, a chubby girl born by an emergency C-section did not change her life, but did get her a nice apartment near the beach.*

12. *Luana is high, drunk, who knows for how many days. The baby is hungry, hot, with one-, or two-, or three-day-old diapers. The baby cries and cries in her cradle until grandparents, who haven't heard from Luana for a few days, find it. "The baby needs love, attention, care," the grandparents say. Luana shrugs.*

13. *Luana says goodbye to her baby at the airport. The grandparents decide to sell their house and start a new life on the mainland for the baby's sake. The island, which is a paradise to so many people, became a living hell because of Luana.*

14. *No one chooses hell if you can be elsewhere.*

15. *Luana hasn't had any other babies. She has had a couple of apartments, jobs, stints in rehab, surfboards, boyfriends, lovers, even a husband, maybe therapists. Ups and downs.*

APRIL 4TH

I don't like talking about Luana, but as I re-read the last few pages, I noticed I have done nothing but write about her. Truth: I do wanna talk to her. It's not that I miss her, it's just that I wonder what life would be like with an actual mother. You could say I'm curious about her.

I know she is a nut case, yes, but her nuttiness has given her a lot of experiences. Can you imagine? She's done it all: alcohol, drugs, rehab, jail. And from a more interesting perspective, she has traveled the world, hitchhiking, backpacking, you name it.

Having seen and lived so much must have taught her a couple of lessons. See, I hate to admit it, but I believe that if there's someone in my family who would understand and respect who I am, it is Luana. That, my friends, is a great tragedy. I bet she would accept me as I am. But of course, first she would have to admit that I am her daughter. Wait, I am not saying she denies me, she simply doesn't acknowledge me in her life.

Having a queer kid can't be as bad as having an addict, right? I have thought about using that line with my grandparents, if they freak out whenever I decide to come out. I can say, "It's not like I am a junkie like your daughter." But that would be low and mean, and they don't deserve either.

But, as I was telling you. I feel that if I wanted to, I could talk to Luana. I have had fantasies in which Luana stops being Luana and becomes Mother.

Did you ever watch *Lilo and Stitch?* Well, Luana looks like Lilo's sister. She is a mess just like her, only Lilo's sister did everything she could to give Lilo a good life. As you can imagine, it's one of my favorite movies of all time for many obvious reasons. Watching it became my first step into the

Hawaiian green life. Before *Lilo and Stitch,* I had only a blurry memory of it all. Also, I didn't care all that much about my Hawaiian heritage before I watched it.

This is how my life is compared to Lilo's:

Lilo was born in Hawaii.	Mikala was born in Hawaii.
Lilo is an orphan who lives with Nani, her sister who is her only relative in the world.	Mikala is not an orphan, but she feels like one. She lives with her only relatives in the US.
Lilo likes Elvis Presley (an icon for Lesbos, says Soledad)	Mikala likes Rufus Wainwright (who is an icon for queers, period).
Lilo has Stitch, a weird creature not from this planet.	Mikala has Soledad, a weird creature not from this planet.
Lilo loves Hawaii.	Mikala loves Hawaii.
Lilo lives in Hawaii.	Mikala wants to live in Hawaii.

APRIL 5ᵀᴴ

So, I finally talked to Luana. She is sober. (I wanted to say to her, "What, for the hundredth time in your life?") She told me she's been going to therapy for the last two years. She says she is working out many aspects of her life. ("Good for you," I wanted to say.) She told me that she's planning to come over during the summer, to see *me*. Me.

I was speechless. I'm not sure what I said after that, but I know that I ended the call by saying, "Hey, I'm doing this homework for chemistry. Can we talk some other time?"

Was that very assholy of me?

I have mixed feelings about Luana. So many that they don't fit in my room. I wanna see her. I wanna be normal and have a normal mother. At the same time, I hate her, I don't want to see her, because well, she hasn't done anything too motherly in the last seventeen years of my life. Plus, I'm afraid of seeing her. What if I like her? What if she leaves again?

APRIL 5TH NIGHT

Soledad just added Tracy, Gina and Frieda to Facebook. She told me she had suggested me as their friend, too. I like Gina and Tracy, but I really really, really, (have I said REALLY?) like Frieda.

APRIL 7TH

Today in my Creative Writing class, Miss Moore made us read a poem by Sylvia Plath; it's called *Daddy*. I am not exaggerating when I say that every single person in class had a "What-the-fuck" face after we read it aloud. Each of us had a turn reading a stanza. I had to read the last one, and believe me when I say that I almost broke down and cried when I finished: "Daddy, daddy, you bastard, I'm through." In my life, this might as well have been, "Mommy, mommy, you bastard, I'm through."

When we finished, we all stayed silent, awed at Plath's poem. Miss Moore then started writing on the board, "In your team, discuss what the poem is abou . . . " She hadn't even finished writing when Soledad said, "That's easy, it's about how she wanted to kill her father, but couldn't."

I turned to look at her, because she sits behind me, and mouthed to her, "You ass," Sole simply shrugged.

Miss Moore, who has the patience that the rest of the world lacks, asked Soledad to see beyond that. She told us all, "Don't take the easy road to get to the meaning of the poem, go deeper." Sometimes we teens don't like to go deeper.

So tonight I have to work on two assignments, 1) What is the revelation in Plath's poem? 2) Write a poem about a personal revelation.

Help needed.

P.S. Frieda accepted to be my friend. Oh, Reader, if you only saw her photos. She is gorgeous. If I invested as much time in my poem as I do on Facebook or on writing to you in this diary, I would have an epic lesbian poem already.

April 8th

I'm thinking that maybe, just maybe, my personal revelation poem might turn into my coming out poem.

Maybe, just *maybe*. For now I have this list of tentative titles:

- *Take me out.*
- *I, Māhū.*
- *Empty My Closet.*
- *Girl likes girls.*
- *Girl out.*

April 8th Night

I have writer's block.

Fine, having a writer's block is way too fancy. So, I may as well say it, I am afraid of writing this poem.

April 9th

I was supposed to submit the first draft of my poem today, but I didn't. It's not finished so I talked to Miss Moore after class and I showed her what I did (I wrote a stanza and a half.) I explained to her what I was trying to do with it. She looked at me and said, "Coming up with a poem is already difficult, now a poem about coming out, well, that must be even more difficult." Did I just come out to my teacher?

Before I left she advised me to feel free to talk to her whenever I wanted, "You know, I'm here for you beyond literature-related issues."

I don't know why she said it, but it felt really nice.

She told me to read Elizabeth Bishop's poems. She said we will do some exercises with her writing next week. "I call them appropriation exercises," she said. I'm curious. Soledad was right, Miss Moore always gives us the most challenging-weird-interesting assignments. A few weeks ago we had to invent a story that started with the following line: "I am a shoe, I am an old stinky left shoe . . ." My shoe was bipolar.

APRIL 9TH LATE NIGHT

Tracy, Gina and Frieda are hanging out with us next weekend. We agreed on meeting at Point Pleasant Beach. I still believe it's too cold to go to the beach, but oh well. I have a lesbo gang, isn't that great? Plus I'm seeing Frieda again, I'm happy.

APRIL 11TH NIGHT

Elizabeth Bishop is wonderful, I have a poetic crush on her. I'm sorry, Sylvia Plath, Bishop's eyes and words have my heart now. I have to thank Miss Moore for recommending her.

APRIL 11TH NIGHT NIGHT

Poems by Elizabeth Bishop that I Like the Most:

- *One Art*
- *A Miracle for Breakfast*
- *The Moose*
- *While Someone Telephones*
- *The Shampoo*

A PRIL 12TH

I've liked Miss Moore since day one; when she gave us the official reading list for the class, she told us she also had an unofficial list. You know, a list with books we are not supposed to read because they are banned.

Excerpt from Miss Moore's Lecture on Official and Unofficial Lists of Books

"I hope you enjoy what I chose for you to read this semester. I had some other authors in mind, but some of them are banned. I wouldn't want you to read banned books even though these banned books are the most wonderful pieces of literature. I have included them in this unofficial list, but I cannot officially give you the unofficial list. I cannot make you read what is included in it, but if any of you are unofficially interested in reading this unofficial list that doesn't officially exist, you are officially invited to ask me for it."

Of course, some of the kids in my class ignored this, but there were some who were actually more interested in this unofficial list than in the other one. Me, for example. What's more seductive than the word *banned*? Tell me *banned* movies, and I wanna watch it, tell me *banned* books, and I wanna read them. I would eat *banned* sushi, I swear. I was the first one to ask her for this list, and we hit it off right away.

Anyway, that is how we sorta started our friendship, Miss Moore and I. She knows me well, I mean, I pretty much came out to her when she read my draft.

Dialogue with Miss Moore About Books and More

Me: Can you recommend something else to read? I love poetry, you know that, but I kinda want to read a novel.

Miss Moore: Sure. First, tell me, what would you

say is the one book you could read at least once a year?

Me: *The Catcher in the Rye*, of course.

Miss Moore: Oh, I believe that's banned in Utah.

Me: Really?

Miss Moore: I don't know for sure, but I wouldn't be surprised. OK, that helps me, you should try *Dora: A Headcase* by Lidia Yuknavitch. Think of it as the female contemporary version of *The Catcher in the Rye*.

Miss Moore also mentioned that the protagonist happens to have a huge crush on one of her girl friends. Also, she likes recording and editing audio and videos. Yes, Reader, Dora is a bit like me. That's why Miss Moore wants me to read it.

One thing led to another and we continued talking about parents and kids and life. I ended up telling her how Luana has been trying to make contact. She was curious about it. "What do you think she wants?" Miss Moore asked.

"No idea," I said.

The rest of the conversation went like this:

Me: But that's not what I wanted to talk to you about.

Miss Moore: I'm all ears. Is this about your revelation poem?

Me: Yeah, sorta. You did understand that I am the one coming out in my poem, right?

Miss Moore: Mmh, I thought so, but I respect your privacy.

Me: Thank you.

Miss Moore: I am honored that you confided in me, and I must tell you that I understand a little bit about what you are going through.

To tell you the truth, I thought she was gonna say, "Because I am gay too." But no, Miss Moore isn't gay.

Miss Moore: My youngest brother, he's twenty-one and, well, he's gay. He came out just a few years ago. It wasn't easy for him.

Me: Were your parents tough on him?

Miss Moore: No, it's more like he was tough on

himself. We accepted it way more than he did. I don't know if you can understand me. I guess, what I'm trying to say, Mikala, is that it's beautiful that you, being so young, are capable of accepting who you are.

Yes, Reader, I officially came out to her. Like, *really* came out. I told Miss Moore about my queerness. It's the first time I've talked about *it* with an adult. It was both strange and comfortable at the same time. I wanted to cry. I didn't dare tell her how inside the closet I actually am.

Before I left she asked what I wanted to do after finishing high school. I didn't even blink—I went all crazy and told her about taking a year off.

Miss Moore: A year off? And what will you do?

Mikala: I wanna go to Hawaii. I wanna live in Hawaii at least for a year; who knows, maybe I'll like it so much that I'll stay for college.

Miss Moore: Hawaii, huh? Every time I hear a student talking about taking a year off after high school I think there's something behind it.

Something they're trying to find. So, I wonder, Mikala, what are you looking for?

I honestly didn't know what to tell her. I mean, all this time I thought I knew why I wanted to go to Hawaii, but I went blank. Is it about going and being as queer as I want? Is it about finding my roots? Is it about Luana? Is it about being independent?

I shrugged at Miss Moore's question.

Miss Moore: Perhaps you don't know what you're looking for. Maybe you'll find that over there, too. Anyway, how's that poem coming along?

Me: I'm not sure.

Miss Moore: Well, keep working on it.

Me: Will do. Oh, by the way, I loved Elizabeth Bishop's poems. Thank you for recommending her to me.

Miss Moore: You know, she lived in Brazil for a very long time. That landscape was a big influence in her writing.

Me: Really?

Miss Moore: Yes, and she liked girls.

Me: Seriously?

Miss Moore: Yup.

I like my teacher, she is awesome. Before I left she asked me about Soledad. It's funny, she thought she and I were kind of a couple. I can see where that comes from. We are always together, and we are always close. (So much that she kicked us out of her class once because we wouldn't stop talking.)

Me: No, Sole and I are only friends. Best friends.

Miss Moore: I see.

Part of me wanted to tell her about Frieda, but it's too soon for that. I have only seen her once (in real life, of course, because I've been stalking her on Facebook).

APRIL 11TH

Today at dinner my grandparents were asking if I had made a decision about Luana's plan.

Me: Her plan?

Grandparents: Yes.

Grandfather: You know, her plan of coming here.

Grandmother: We want you to know that we'll respect you if you decide to say yes, but—and I'm speaking for both of us—we believe it's best if she doesn't come.

Me: Well, I haven't really thought about it. I dunno how serious she is about coming. If I do decide I want her to come and visit, would you get mad?

Grandfather: Well, no.

Me: But?

Grandfather: No buts, it's just that . . .

Grandmother: It's just that we are afraid of her cancelling at the very last minute and breaking your heart.

Me: She wouldn't break my heart. At this point, I don't expect anything from her. What do I have to lose?

Grandfather: You see, even you know this isn't a good idea.

Me: That's not what I said. You know? I dunno

how I feel about the whole thing. She's saying she's going to rehab and therapy. She says she's changed. Maybe she has, just a little.

Both of them faked a smile and nodded. It's so easy to read them, they don't want Luana here.

What if Luana did come? What if the trip actually was a good idea and she and I, well, we get to bond like never before?

Oh, Luana, you are not here and still you are here (in case you wonder, I am pointing to my head).

CHAPTER SIX
frenemies

A PRIL 13TH
      Tomorrow I am seeing Frieda. Tomorrow
I am seeing Frieda. Tomorrow I am seeing Frieda.
Tomorrow I am seeing Frieda. Tomorrow I am
seeing Frieda. Tomorrow I am seeing Frieda.

A PRIL 13TH NOON
      Title: HAWAIIAN FEVER

ACT 2

INTERIOR OF A HOTEL ROOM.

The sounds of the waves fill the room. Close-up to a canopy bed where two bodies are moving under the covers. Some moaning can be heard.

Frieda (Off Screen Voice): Yes, oh, yes, right there, right there.
Frieda (Off Screen Voice): Mikala, you are wonderful. You are . . .

How the fuck am I supposed to write a sex scene if I have never even had sex? I know now that touching your own pussy does not count as sex. Not even if you do it next to your best friend. If it did count, then you and I know I have had sex, but it's obviously not as hot as it would be to *actually* do it with someone.

Someone like Frieda, of course.

Soledad sent me a link to a website which offers this kind of interactive manual for lesbian sex. It's funny, really. On one side you have a list of verbs, and with the cursor you choose one then place it in whichever part of the body of this blonde chick who is in the middle of the screen. She makes sounds and everything.

Yeah, my sex education is coming from a girl who is a virgin like me and from the fucking internet. My life, my sex life, is pretty pathetic.

OK, all this sex talk is warming me up. I should, you know, have some quality time with myself. Some pussy-touchy will also help me release stress. (I have a stash of coconut oil under my bed. Yes, the same thing Grandma uses for cooking works as lube!)

APRIL 13TH AFTERNOON

OH MY GOD! I just had the most embarrassing moment. I closed the computer, turned off the lights in my room and left on only the night table lamp. You can say I was creating a romantic mood for myself. (Oh, come on, I'm sure you have probably done it yourself.)

Anyway, I got in bed and started caressing my

tummy (yes, with the coconut oil, of course.) It might sound stupid but the smell and texture of the coconut oil brings such a soothing feeling, it gives me goose bumps, it gets me in the mood. (It's kinda become a problem when Grandma cooks with coconut oil, because instead of thinking about food I think about masturbation.)

Anyway, there we were, my coconut oil, my hand, and me, having fun. And just as I started going below my belly, *pum*, the door opens. It was my grandmother.

I jumped my ass off the bed. She obviously didn't see anything bad, because really I wasn't doing shit (yet).

Grandma: Ikaika is here. What are you doing? Is that my coconut oil on your night table?

Me: I was about to take a nap, and no, it's not your coconut oil. I got some. I read somewhere that it's excellent for dry skin.

Grandma: You had to read that in order to believe it? I've been telling you, coconut oil is good for everything: skin, hair, food. Anyway, get dressed, Mika. You don't want Ikaika to see you like that.

Ikaika. I haven't seen him much since NYC. I wonder what he wants, he never comes without calling or texting first.

APRIL 13ᵀᴴ NIGHT

My poor boyfriend is broken-hearted, and not even by me. Tom-Tom gave him an ultimatum, either Ikaika comes out or they can't continue together. "It's a matter of principle," Tom-Tom stated. I understand what he means. He's very open about his life, but he should know by now how different that is from Ikaika's situation.

Ikaika says he can't do it. I understand him. I would feel exactly the same if I were in his place. I honestly envy how open some people can be about their sexuality, but at the same time, I know every situation is different. And Ikaika's and mine are very similar. Our families are too traditional, and coming out would mean breaking them apart. (At least that's how I feel about my grandparents, in Ikaika's case, his father would be the one breaking Ikaika apart.)

To cheer him up I invited him to the beach with the girls. He said "maybe," and then asked me if that *special someone* was coming, too.

Ikaika and Mikala's Dialogue about a Certain Girl

Me: Who?

Ikaika: The girl you haven't told me about.

Me: I dunno what you are talking about.

Ikaika: You do. I can tell one of your new friends stole your heart.

Me: Shut up.

Of course I ended up telling my "boyfriend" all about Frieda. At least that distracted him from his own shit.

Ikaika: Well, now I wanna meet this Frieda. Hey, and what does Soledad think?

Me: About what?

Ikaika: About you liking someone other than her.

Me: You, too? Why does everyone think there's something between Soledad and me? We are just FRIENDS.

Ikaika: Oh, no, girl. I don't think there's something between you guys. I gotta tell you this, and don't take this the wrong way, I like Soledad, but . . .

Me: But?

Ikaika: She is VERY possessive. She acts as if you were hers.

Me: What are you talking about?

Ikaika: Look, before this thing with Tom-Tom, he told me Soledad came up to him and, well, she asked him . . . no, she stated that she found it weird how close you and I were. You follow me? As if there was something between you and me.

Me: You're kidding.

Ikaika: No, I'm not. I would say ask Tom-Tom, but now is not the time to ask him anything.

Tom-Tom thinks Soledad was trying to say: "Tell your boyfriend to leave my girl alone."

Me: Huh, well, yeah, maybe Sole can be a bit . . .

Ikaika: Controlling?

Me: I was gonna say greedy when it comes to attention, but yeah, I guess controlling also fits her.

Ikaika: I think she invented the word, ha ha.

Me: It's good to see you laughing.

Ikaika: It's easy with you. Oh Mikala, thank you for listening to me. I love that you're my "girlfriend."

When he left, he hugged me. We stayed there for a while. I told him, "Ikaika, I love having you in my life." Now, the funny thing is that my grandma saw us, she even probably heard us. I noticed smiling and sighing. So now, she probably thinks I just found the love of my life at age seventeen, just like she did. It wouldn't surprise me if she started talking to us about getting married.

APRIL 13TH VERY LATE AT NIGHT

I was dreaming I was in bed with Frieda, and we were doing it. Suddenly someone opened the door and caught us in the act. I didn't recognize this person, but I know I felt very embarrassed.

Dreaming of being caught while having sex is like dreaming you are naked in front of your whole class, right?

I think so.

APRIL 14TH

I went to Soledad's so we could go together to the beach. It took her ages to get ready. "We're just going to the beach," I groaned, but she ignored me. So I started reading my diary (I like reading old entries and imagine you reading them.) Then I started texting Ikaika; Soledad got a bit mad. "Who are you texting?" she asked. "Oh, don't tell me: your *boyfriend.*" Our conversation turned a bit weird (yes, again).

Weird Dialogue with Soledad

Me: It's like you're mad that I'm texting him. You just made the same face you always make when I tell you I'm meeting him. What's wrong? Don't you like him?

Soledad: It's not that I don't like him.

Me: I invited him to the beach.

Soledad: You did? You didn't tell me.

Me: I didn't think *I had to*. Anyway, he's not coming.

Soledad: Oh. That's too bad, but maybe it's best. It was supposed to be an *all-girl* day out. Gina, Tracy, you, me, and Frieda.

Frieda. Frieda. I'm nervous. I feel butterflies in my belly (and below my belly). I am finally seeing Frieda.

A PRIL 14TH NIGHT
Man, I don't understand women. What was supposed to be an awesome day at the beach turned into something pretty weird. Gina and Tracy

were arguing the whole time. Frieda ignored us and sat down on her own to read a book. Soledad was flirting-checking out a group of guys playing volleyball on the beach.

I was bored to death and toasting myself under the sun. At some point Frieda yelled, "Oh, my god, she didn't!" We were all like, "what the fuck?" But Gina and Tracy went back to their own shit, and I couldn't help myself and approached Frieda.

Me: That book has got you hooked, eh?

Frieda: You have no idea, have you read it? It's *Sharp Objects* by Gillian Flynn. It's a mystery/thriller kinda thing. Well, the mother of the protagonist, she . . .

Me: Oh, no. No spoilers, please.

Frieda: It's great. It's so dark.

Me: Flynn, isn't she the author of *Gone Girl?*

Frieda: Yeah, you know it?

Me: Well, I have it, but I haven't even started it. Grandma got it for me, because she says everyone's talking about it.

Frieda: Let's make a deal, read *Gone Girl* and then when you're done with that and I'm done with this we can exchange books.

Me: Sounds like a plan. ·

Frieda: So, you like reading?

Me: A lot.

Frieda and I got so into talking, she forgot about her own book and before I knew it, we were both talking about authors, books, movies. Then at some point, Soledad turned to us just to make fun. She went, "Oh my god, girls, we are at the beach, we are here to look gorgeous and flirt, not be fucking nerds."

I pretended I didn't care, but I did. Soledad can be a real bitch sometimes. Frieda must have noticed something, cause she said, "Soledad, not all of us came to hunt," and then she turned to me to continue talking about Patricia Highsmith's books. Soledad did not snap back, which is kinda weird.

She lay on the sand for a while, then she sat up

again and yelled, "Mika, Mika, come check out that girl, she's totally your type." She pointed at some super butchy girl with a boy haircut and muscles that would give anyone the chills. Not my type, for sure.

I didn't say anything. Everyone around looked at me. I stood up and went for a walk. When I came back everyone was napping except for Frieda, who was back in her book. Our lesbo sunny day in the beach turned into a boring day with too much sand inside my bikini.

APRIL 14ᵀᴴ VERY LATE AT NIGHT
Frieda was in my dreams, again. She was so beautiful. We were making out. French kissing, touching, hands everywhere. This time no one opened the door, this time we had a chance to *you know*.

When I woke up I was, oh my, I am ashamed to say it, I was . . . I was wet, soaking wet.

Yeah, Mikala had a wet dream, geez!

APRIL 15TH

Today in the computer lab, instead of working on our essays, Soledad and me started chatting. Don't give me that look, I'm sure you have done the same sometime in your life. You know, you open a document, pretend to write in it when your teacher is around, but actually you're in the iChat catching up with someone.

Soledad: What is up with Frieda?

Me: What do you mean?

Soledad: Do you like her or what?

Me: Why you ask?

Soledad: Cause if you don't, I might be interested.

Me: You might or you are?

Soledad: I think I am and I was planning to ask her out, but I didn't wanna do it before you know, talking to you.

Me: Well, it seems like you already have a plan.

Soledad: You don't mind then? You know I wouldn't do anything that might hurt you. It's just, I dunno, I think she might like *me*, and it's flattering.

Yup. That's my friend Soledad, her ego is the size of Texas. I love her, but geez.

Do you think I should've told her that I sorta have a semi-crush on Frieda? Please don't say yes, 'cause I didn't. I said nothing. I should've, right?

I can be such a moron sometimes.

April 15TH Night

I called Ikaika to see how he was doing. He's still sad, obviously, but he refused to tell me more about it. He wanted gossip from the beach. Anything that would take him out of his personal drama. I told him about Frieda and me talking about books until Soledad turned into a bitch.

Ikaika: Honey, your friend was a bitch already.

Me: Don't say that!

Ikaika was quiet.

Me: Only I get to say that. She's not a bitch,

she's a total fucking bitch. You were right, it's like the second she sees she's not my center of attention, or *the* center of attention, period, she loses it.

Ikaika: I told you.

Me: Yeah, man. I don't know what to do, but that's not the worst part.

Ikaika: There's more?

Me: She wants to ask her out.

Ikaika: What?

Me: Yes, Soledad asked me if I was interested in Frieda.

Ikaika: Tell me you told her you had a big fat crush on that girl.

Me: She didn't even give me a chance.

Ikaika: Mikala, you gotta tell her you have feelings for Frieda.

Me: I know, I know. But I don't know if what is inside me are actually *feelings*. How do you know if you are in love? How can you tell between a simple crush and love?

Ikaika: You just know.

When I hung up with Ikaika I came to the conclusion that yes, I gotta tell Soledad that I have
a tiny crush on Frieda. I mean, she's not really
that interested in her, anyway. Plus, if I don't and
things work out between them I am gonna feel
weird. Not that I believe I have a chance with
Frieda, but Soledad is *my* best friend and I owe
her honesty.

That's what she always says, best friends tell each
other everything. Not to tell her would be like lying,
and I already do enough of that with my grandparents, right?

Anyway, Ikaika and I are having dinner tomorrow. We're going to get sloppy joes at Gigio's, the
best in town. If eating sloppy joes at Gigio's doesn't
cheer him up, then we're lost. It's a school night,
and my grandparents normally don't let me go out
on a school night, but since it will be a "date" with
Ikaika, I'm sure they'll say yes.

APRIL 16TH

It's official. I am a loser. I tried to talk to Soledad, you know, open up about Frieda, but before I got to say anything she told me she spent the night chatting with her.

APRIL 17TH

~~Once upon a time, in a faraway kingdom there were two princesses.~~ Once upon a time in one small Hawaiian island, there were two girls. They did everything together. They would braid each other's hair, they would choose carefully one flower after the other to make the most wonderful and perfumed garland for each other's necks. They would ~~dance hula~~ surf together, too. They were the best in town.

The two girls grew up and turned into beautiful ~~tall~~ women. Their skin was tanned and golden, their hair was long and black. Everyone envied them. They promised themselves to be friends forever, no matter what.

But one day, an evil demon in the form of a woman came to their lives and . . .

This is stupid. I should stop writing forever and ever. I'm fucking sad. Soledad is seeing Frieda this weekend. Plus, I didn't get to go out with Ikaika, Grandma said no. Can you believe it? She says I'm seeing Ikaika way too much; she said there must be some limits. "I don't want you coming home one day telling me he knocked you up."

I almost laughed out loud.

APRIL 17TH NIGHT

OMG, you won't believe what just happened. I decided to log in to Facebook before going to bed. Aaaaaaand, I chatted with Frieda. Yes, with FRIEDA! This is how it went:

Frieda: Hey, Mikala, you there?

Mikala: Frieda, what up?

Frieda: Oh, I'm so glad you're online.

Mikala: Me, why?

Frieda: It's kinda embarrassing; it's about your friend Soledad.

Mikala: What about her?

I have to be honest. My insides were in pain, I was so, so, so sure that Frieda was gonna say, "I love her, I love Soledad. I love her so much that my skin hurts, help me." I was ready for that; I was ready to suck it up. But instead,

Frieda: She asked me out, as in "let's go out on a date." Mikala, it was just so weird. I can't explain it, but it's like she tricked me into not being able to say no. It doesn't make sense, I know. I don't like her, I mean, not like that.

Reader, can you imagine my face? :) :) :) :)

Mikala: Believe me, I totally understand you. Soledad has her ways with words. It happens to me all the time. I think one of these days she is gonna talk me into robbing a bank.

Frieda: Ha, ha, you betcha.

Mikala: So, what ya gonna do?

Frieda: Well, I have a HUGE favor to ask you.

Mikala: Shoot.

Frieda: Join us.

Mikala: What do you mean?

Frieda: Come with us.

Mikala: But, it's a date. I can't go with you guys.

Frieda: Just leave that up to me. I have every-thing planned.

Mikala: Walk me through it.

Frieda: Well, she wants to go out on Saturday, and I gotta help my mother at the flea market. I did tell you she sells vintage stuff, didn't I?

Mikala: No, but that sounds amazing.

Frieda: Well, why don't you come to the flea market, "run into me." We can hang out there and then we go together and meet Soledad.

Mikala: Are you sure?

Frieda: Yes, anyway, I was already considering invit-ing you over. It's my mother's habit to disappear and leave me there in charge all by myself. I normally just stay there and read or text or Facebook just to pass the time. But if you come we can continue our book club.

Mikala: Well, that sounds . . .

Frieda: Like a date? Perfect, it's all set. (Did you notice how I just *Soledad-ed* you into it?)

Mikala: Totally.

A PRIL 19TH
List of Things to Do Today

- *Clean my room.*
- *Do my homework*
- *Take a shower.*
- *Go to the flea market and meet Frieda*
- *Frieda, Frieda, Frieda.*
- *Third-wheel Frieda and Soledad's date in the evening.*

A PRIL 19TH NIGHT
Summary of the Day

- *Soledad hates me.*
- *Soledad hates me.*
- *Soledad hates me.*

Today things went good and bad, or should I say too good and too bad. Let me expand on this:

The Too-Good: The flea market and Frieda's stall. Her mom has amazing stuff for sale, vintage-kitsch accessories and clothing, which obviously attracts the weirdest people. So our book club/girl chat turned into people watching. I have never laughed so hard. We also got to know more about each other. Frieda told me about her issues with her mom. "It's like she thinks we can be friends who tell each other everything. Can you believe her?" She says she would rather live full time with her dad.

I told her I don't live with my mom, and that obviously she's not trying to be friends with me. Sharing experiences is nice. Her mom is very cool, so I don't really understand why they don't get along. She told me that if I ever needed a job she would gladly hire me. (To this Frieda said, "or you could actually pay a salary to your daughter.") At four-ish we went to the coffee shop where Soledad was waiting for Frieda, and so I can now tell you about . . .

The Too-Bad: Soledad shit her pants when she saw me coming in with Frieda. Frieda offered her nicest voice to say, "Look who I ran into? I invited her so the three of us can gossip together."

There was nothing for Soledad to say except for a very fake, "That's great."

As you can imagine Soledad tried to capture Frieda's attention all afternoon. She would only address me to say things like, "Remember, Mikala how everyone complimented me for my outfit/hair/poem/song/etc.? Or she would come up with anecdotes that would make me look like an ass (sadly, there are many of those).

At some point Frieda went to the bathroom and Soledad went, "Why are *you* here?" I re-told Frieda's story, but it didn't matter, Sole was mad. "But you knew I had asked her on a date." I had nothing to add. I could tell she was fucking mad at me. When Frieda came back from the bathroom things got worse, but this time for Soledad because Frieda did everything in her power to make the day about me, about us. Her whole attention was on me.

I am surprised Soledad did not throw her hot cup of coffee at me.

A PRIL 19TH MIDNIGHT
Frieda and I chatted for almost an hour.

Frieda: Mikala, you there? Frieda calling Mikala. Mikala please respond.

Mikala: Hey, hey, hey, didn't I just say good-bye to you like an hour ago?

Frieda: Well, yes, but I already miss you.

Dear Reader, please insert a sigh here and a bunch of happy faces.

Mikala: Yeah, I'm very *missable*.

Frieda: Miserable? Why? Because Soledad was such a bitch with you?

Mikala: I said missable, but yeah, can you believe her? I thought she was gonna punch me in the face.

Frieda: Me too. Anyway, Tracy just texted me.

Mikala: Uh huh?

Frieda: Do you have plans next weekend?

Mikala: Not really, I am still going over *this* weekend. Why?

Frieda: Tracy and Gina, they have a game.

Mikala: Game?

Frieda: Yes, those butches are on the basketball team from school. You didn't know?

Mikala: No.

Frieda: Oh, well, they're great. Those two are like the stars of the team. Actually, that's how they became friends or whatever they are.

Mikala: There's something between them, right?

Frieda: Yes, they just won't admit it, who knows why. Anyway, do you wanna come? I promise it'll be fun.

Mikala: Yes.

Frieda: Cool, I will let you both know when and where the game is. Now, I gotta go, talk to you later!

APRIL 21ST

Picture this. Monday. Soledad and me in school. She wearing mini-shorts, the kind that get her in trouble with our teachers, high boots, and a flowery t-shirt. Me, jeans, purple converse and a white t-shirt with the letters F*CK Y*U in bright pink. We are ten or fifteen steps from each other. Face to face. The school disappears and it turns into an old western town. Horses and people around us. She looks at me, I look at her. We approach each other. We *hey* each other. Neither of us dares to take the gun out. She says,

Soledad: Sooooo, Frieda and you did something fun this Sunday?

Me: No, well, I didn't see her, but we've been texting and you can say that was fun.

Soledad: Well, good for you.

Me: Sole, if you have something to say, just say it.

Soledad: What're you talking about?

Me: About me, showing up with Frieda on Saturday, to *your* date.

Soledad: It wasn't a date, is that what she told you? Oh my, that Frieda is so full of herself. I said I'd have coffee with her just because.

Me: Wait, what? She invited you? I heard *you* had invited her. You had asked *her* out.

Soledad: Oh, so I'm lying now?

Me: No, no, that's not what I said.

Soledad: Whatever. Anyway, I don't know if you heard but Tracy and Gina are playing this weekend, you wanna go?

Me: Oh, yeah, that's on Saturday, isn't it?

Soledad: Yes, how do you . . . ?

Me: Frieda told me, actually, she invited me.

Soledad: Oh.

Me: Soledad, I think we should talk about this.

Soledad: Talk about what? The game? I'm just going because Tracy invited me.

Me: *(thinking about Tracy inviting Soledad)*

Soledad: What's with that face?

Me: Nothing.

Soledad: You sure?

Me: Yup.

Soledad: So, I got class. I'll see you later, I guess.

Me: I guess.

A PRIL 22ND AT LUNCH
Soledad: So, there's something I haven't told you, Mika.

Me: One, Don't call me Mika, you know I hate it. Two, what haven't you told me?

Soledad: I blush just to think about it. Oh my god, Mikala, I had cybersex, CYBERSEX, can you believe it? Have you ever had cybersex? Of course you haven't, you would've told me already, right? Cause you and me, we tell each other everything. Anyway it was fucking AMAZING, oh my god Mikala, I think I'm in love.

Me: Who did you have cybersex with?

Soledad: Oh, you don't know this person.

Me: This person? Can you be more vague?

Soledad: I would give you details, but what if you end up dating my person instead of me? Ha ha ha. Ay, don't make that face, I am kidding.

What did I say? Nothing, I stood there and smiled. My guess? Soledad is lying. What do you think? I don't understand why though.

APRIL 25TH

The game is tomorrow. Sole and I were supposed to go together, but she just texted me that she might not go because she's, "Got stuff to do."

I called Ikaika right away and told him about the whole thing. His words? "Sole is being an asshole. For the first time she's not the center of attention and she can't stand it."

He's right.

Soledad and I have been friends 'til now, 'cause now we are more like *frenemies*.

One should not be in the position of choosing between your friend and your significant one. But now that I'm into this, I have decided to fight for the girl I like.

April 26TH

Soledad has just texted. She is going to the game after all . . . No wait, let's be more accurate. She texted saying, I'm going to the game with Frieda, u?

The war has begun.

April 26TH Night

List of Things to Do Tomorrow

- Take a long bath
- Shave my legs
- Wax my mustache
- Pluck my eyebrows
- Wish for the best.

CHAPTER SEVEN
mad for her

Ap PRIL 26ᵀᴴ

Hudson County. — Mikala Kekoa hit a three-pointer at the buzzer to give herself a 10-5 upset victory over Soledad Bäcker at a love game played over Frieda Gaherty before a sellout crowd of who knows how many teens at the Memorial High School Gym last Saturday.

The first half featured several lead changes with neither of the girls gaining momentum because Frieda Gaherty was too busy cheering for her friends Miss Tracy Jones and Miss Gina Bellinim who were later sent to the bench because of some argument with the rival team.

But then Kekoa took a one-point lead at half-time, as she offered to braid Gaherty's hair. Bäcker battled back to tie the game by offering reflexology on Gaherty's left hand, holding Kekoa off for nearly ten minutes. Then, Kekoa built a five-point lead at 5:10, as Miss Frieda Gaherty leaned on Kekoa's shoulder. Soledad Bäcker's game went to hell because she decided to get Gaherty a soda and a tray of nachos.

Both teams suffered from shooting woes as Frieda Gaherty went to the bathroom and stayed there for almost twenty minutes talking to some former classmate.

Kekoa opened the second half as she offered her jacket to Gaherty, who was presumably cold. This gave Kekoa a six-point lead. Soledad Bäcker then tried to use the old strategy of I-can-make-you-warm, highlighted by a hug, but Gaherty refused as she started cheering again for her friends playing in the actual game.

The lead changed hands three more times before Kekoa built a five-point advantage as Gaherty leaned on her shoulder again. Bäcker battled back, *but it was too late, Gaherty and Kekoa were already holding hands and giggling with each other. Game over.*

A PRIL 27TH

I

am

in

LOVE

A PRIL 27TH NIGHT

I spent Sunday afternoon working at the Community Garden; my grandparents have a spot there. I invited Ikaika so we could talk about last night's game. I told him how stupid Soledad and

I acted, competing for Frieda's attention, but how surprising it was that somehow I won the girl.

Seriously, Frieda was nice to me, laughing at my stupid jokes, and everything. She wasn't rude or anything with Soledad. It was just clear that she was being friendly with her and more, more, MORE attentive to me.

Wait, I got something else to tell you, Reader.

You ready?

Frieda kissed me goodbye.

Yup, she kissed *me*.

It was a soft, tender kiss, but a kiss is a kiss.

The only problem is that now I feel kinda shitty because Soledad saw her and she seemed upset the rest of the night. I feel so fucking guilty, and I hate it.

Ikaika was happy for me, the happiest I have seen him in days since he and Tom-Tom broke up. But then he turned serious. He sat me down on the ground, held my hands, and made me promise him that I would not make the same mistake he did.

Excerpt from Ikaika's Lessons at the Community Garden

Ikaika: You must not hide yourself.

Mikala: What do you mean? I'm not hiding, my grandparents know where I am.

Ikaika: You know what I mean, sweetie, you must not hide who you are. It's time you come out to them.

Mikala: Ikaika, you know that is out of the question.

Ikaika: Well it shouldn't be, you must face them.

Mikala: But . . .

Ikaika: No buts, Mikala, you gotta. See what happened to me. I lost the man I love because of my cowardice.

Mikala: I don't know, dude, I would break my grandparents' hearts.

Ikaika: Mikala, your grandparents love you, they will understand. They just want what's best for you, and being honest about yourself is part of that.

Mikala: No, I can't hurt them, they've been through so much already, you know, with Luana.

Ikaika: Stop it. Don't do that to yourself. You are NOTHING like Luana. That should be clear to them by now. You are always comparing yourself to her or bringing her to the conversation even though she's not in your life.

APRIL 28TH EARLY IN THE MORNING

I didn't sleep, thinking about Ikaika's words of wisdom. He was so blunt and honest. He moved me.

Oh Reader, I wish you could talk to me. Do you think I should just come out? Be honest. Should I? Can I? Must I?

APRIL 28TH NIGHT

Today Grandma made Kahlua pig for dinner, my favorite. It's cooked kinda like a pulled pork, but it's served with delicious steamed cabbage. Grandpa prepared some Mai Tai cocktails, he even made a virgin Mai Tai for me. Why? They have the Hawaiian blues, a fever they get a couple times a year.

You see, we don't eat Hawaiian food all that often (except for Spam; we eat that almost every other day). (Yes, in case you wonder, the myth about us Hawaiians eating a lot of Spam is not a myth, it's a reality.) Grandma is a great cook, you give her fish, shrimp, fruit, and she can do wonders. Grandpa's good, too, his *pipikalua* is the best of the best. (I have nothing to compare it with. Maybe their food actually sucks compared to real Hawaiian food.)

After dinner, my grandparents started asking me about my plans for the future.

Me: The future?

Grandparents: Yes, the future.

Grandfather: As in *what are you going to do once you finish high school.*

Me: Isn't it too soon to think about that? I'm still a junior.

Grandma: But next year will be your last in high school, and you need to start planning, sending applications.

Grandpa: We don't even know what it is that you wanna study.

Grandma: You do wanna go to college, right Mika?

Me: Well, I . . . guess, I dunno. I'm kinda lost, actually.

Grandpa: Don't you have dreams?

I'm not lying to them, at least not about college. I really haven't thought about it. All I know is that I wanna go to Hawaii, I wanna live there. At least for a while. But I know that going back to the island is not what they want for me, they would never allow it. But I grew a good pair of balls.

Conversation about Mikala's Dreams

Me: I do, I do have a dreams. I wanna go to Hawaii.

Grandpa: Hawaii?

Grandma: On vacation you mean?

Me: Well, you know, there is something called a gap year. Kids my age take a year off after high school to explore life before going into . . .

Grandpa: Gap year? What are you talking about?

Grandma: Mikala, you wanna end up like your mother?

Me: No, no, no and I HATE it when you say that. I hate it when you talk shit about her.

(Yup, that's what I said, me the nicest granddaughter on earth, the one who never disobeys, the one who always-always-always does what she's told. Yes, me, Mikala Kekoa, started an argument and used the *s* word.)

Grandpa: Mikala, watch your language.

Grandma: Don't yell at her. It's OK. Mikala, what is it? I've never seen you this mad. Is this something that Luana put in your head?

I know, I know I should have continued. I know I should have opened up and said everything that has been stuck on my chest since who knows when. But I couldn't. I should have said that no, it wasn't something Luana put in my head, it's something I put in my head because I wanna experience life. I wanna live a free lesbian life, and while I'm at it, I wanna get to know Luana, *my* mother. But I didn't. I stood up and left.

Grandpa: Mikala, come here. Mikala! Your grandma is talking to you!

I've been in my room for hours now. I haven't even gone to the bathroom. I don't wanna see them. I don't wanna see any of them. I don't want another confrontation. I should have kept my mouth shut. The Kahlua pig grandma cooked starts jumping in my stomach, like it's yelling inside of my belly, saying: Luana, Future, Lesbian.

APRIL 29TH

I looked for Soledad this morning, she's actually the only one I can talk to about my family. But Soledad is not talking to me. She even changed places at our Creative Writing class. I hate it that she's mad without telling me why. Yes, yes, Reader, we both know why she's mad. She's mad that I sorta stole Frieda from her, but she should say so, right?

I know she'll get over it, I'm sure . . . Just give her a few days to find a new love interest and she'll be done. This whole deal with Frieda will be out of her mind. Who knows, maybe there is actually *someone else* keeping her busy and amusing her with cybersex.

Frieda and I, by the way, chatted till late last night. No, I didn't have cybersex with her like Soledad did with her new "someone," but it was great. I think she likes me for reals.

April 29th Night

Tracy's birthday is next weekend. She's having a party at her place. Some of her friends from school and from her team are going, AAAAND she has even invited Gina, Frieda, Soledad and me to spend the night afterwards. I don't know if Soledad is going, but I am. Grandma wasn't too convinced. She *is* talking to me, but I can tell she's still mad at me. In the end, I gave up. I apologized and told her I didn't know why I acted like that. "I'm just lost, Grandma," I said. But I lied, I've been thinking and I know what I want. I want everything: I want my mother, I want Hawaii, I want the girl.

Anyway, apologizing to Grandma got me into going to Tracy's party. The only condition is that Ikaika takes me. "No problem," I said. Now that Soledad is stepping out of my life, Ikaika has become more and more important.

Anyway, Grandma wants to meet my friends. "Or are they imaginary?" she asked. Grandma can be funny. I promised her I would introduce her. "Maybe for your birthday?" she said. That's right, my birthday is soon. I'll be eighteen! I'll ask Grandpa to make us a wonderful Hawaiian dinner; I just need to make sure my friends understand that my grand-parents are "blind to queerness," as Soledad says.

Fucking Soledad, I miss her.

APRIL 30TH

Part of me regrets inviting Ikaika to go shopping. Part of me doesn't. But I really needed an outfit for Tracy's party. I wanna show Frieda I can wear something besides t-shirts and jeans.

Oh, but back to Ikaika. Geez, the only thing he wanted to talk about is coming out. He was so self-deprecating, calling himself a coward. Obviously, he misses Tom-Tom, but I think this is not only about his ex. I've only met his mother, and she seems sweet and kind, the kind of woman who would love her kid no matter what (not that I know that much about that, Luana hasn't called or texted again).

(No, I'm not surprised. Whatever.)

After his long monologue, Ikaika's attention focused in on my own coming out. He insists that I gotta do it. I told him I don't even know if there is actually something going on between Frieda and me. "Don't do it for Frieda, do it for yourself," he said.

He's right, I know.

P.S. I got an amazing pair of skinny jeans and a man's shirt with a bow tie, I am wearing that to the party. I just need a cute pair of black flats, 'cause mine are too old, and I'll be ready.

MAY 1ST

May is here. The best month of the year, yes, my birthday is nearing. Also, I have the feeling that May will bring good fortune to me.

MAY 2ND

Miss Moore gave me back my second draft of my Coming Out poem. She liked it, but believes it is falling short. Like I was not coming *all* out. Surprise, surprise.

When I left the classroom, Soledad was waiting for me outside. "How did it go?" she asked. I was surprised that she was interested. Maybe she got over the fact that Frieda prefers me. I showed her my poem; she read it and asked if she could keep it.

I said, "It's not ready, I have to make some changes that Miss Moore suggested."

We talked about this weekend's party. She said we should go together, which means she really is not mad at me anymore. I explained that I had asked Ikaika to go with me.

She said, "That's OK." I'm happy, I really love Soledad, and it's stupid to fight over a girl.

Before each of us went to our next class she asked me, "Do you like Frieda?" I said yes. "You mad for her?" I said yes. She nodded and smiled, then she said something pretty odd: "Then you can have her."

I didn't say anything, but what the fuck, as if it all depended on her, right? But, Reader, now we are at peace with her. You can stop hating her for me.

CHAPTER EIGHT
māhū love

MAY 3ᴿᴰ
Party-Is-Today. Ikaika is picking me up, then we are getting Soledad, and off we go. Yay!

MAY 4TH AT NOON
I'm back home. I'm too tired to write. I need to take a nap, then, I promise, I promise I will tell you all about last night's party. One thing I can tell you. Someone-got-lucky-last-night.

MAY 4ᵀᴴ AFTERNOON
Tracy's Party, Part 1
Ikaika, Soledad, Jane (yup, Soledad brought a

new friend!), and I arrive at Tracy's. Frieda opens the door. I smile, she smiles. We all smile. Frieda opens her arms for everyone. Soledad introduces her to Jane. (Jane, by the way, is kinda cute, but too serious if you ask me, and very nerdy looking.) But back to me, Frieda hugs me last. She touches my bowtie, caresses my hair, she says, "I'm glad you're here." Soledad, Jane, and Ikaika are already inside.

Frieda holds my hand and walks me in.

Loud music.

Girls. Very tall girls.

Boys. Very skinny and very gay boys.

Dancing.

Food.

Virgin Cocktails.

Tracy's mom going a bit nuts with the noise. Tracy looks amazing. She cut her hair. She is holding hands with Gina. It seems that they finally sorted things out. Tracy's mom seems OK about it.

You haven't lived until you've danced with a

team of very tall basketball players and the girl you like.

Frieda. Frieda wearing a mini-skirt, a pair of flowery Dr. Martens and a see-through black blouse. She takes my hand and invites me to dance with her. Frieda and her skin that smells like French vanilla ice cream. Frieda and her red lips. Frieda and her smile.

Ikaika smiles at me like he's saying, "You go girl." I do everything Frieda wants. I dance, I sit down, I grab a drink, I walk around hand in hand with her. I am so pussy-whipped by her. We dance and dance and dance.

Gina and Tracy have never seemed so happy. Soledad's full attention is on Jane. It's only like twenty people or so in the living room-dining room but it feels like a hundred. We are all having fun. This is the best party ever.

Tracy's Party, Part 2

At midnight, Tracy's mom goes to bed and the

real party starts. Someone pours vodka in the cock-tails. Someone else brings beer from the trunk of a car. Someone else takes out a bong. Gina worries. Tracy swears it's OK. Her mother sleeps like a rock after two Xanax, and she probably had three. We all laugh.

An hour later some of the guests start leaving. More alcohol arrives.

Everyone is now drunk, high, or just very happy to be here, who knows? Tracy and Gina's friends take turns dancing with Soledad who, as always, is the soul of this party. First a boy, then a girl, etc. Ikaika is talking with two guys, one of them seems very interested in him, his hand on Ikaika's shoul-der. We exchange looks, Ikaika smiles for the first time in days.

Me? I don't know when we stopped dancing. I feel dizzy. My last drink had more alcohol than juice. Frieda takes me to the kitchen, I follow her. She sits down on the kitchen counter.

She smiles. She licks her lips. I smile. I lick mine.

We are alone in the kitchen. First, I sit across from her, on the other side of the counter, next to the sink. Some girls come to get ice. One of them turns on the sink to get water and gets me wet. I jump. Frieda laughs and asks me to get close to her. She perches from the counter, her long beautiful legs hanging. She pulls me and I end up standing up between her legs, facing away from her, my arms on her knees.

So far, so good.

I stare at her Dr. Martens. The colors in them, the flowers in them. Her legs, Frieda's awesome legs. People come in and out of the kitchen. We are the only two who remain. I let my hands slide over each one of her legs. She raises her legs and embraces me with them. "You're trapped," she says. I don't say a word. I inch closer to her crotch. My back on her crotch.

Her arms are around my shoulders, her right hand caressing first my neck, then my chin, my lips. Her fingers on my lips. I close my eyes. I can smell her skin, her French vanilla skin. Her face is on the back of my head. She smells my hair and says, "You smell like pineapple." I'm about to explain to her that it's my shampoo, but then she adds, "I wanna bite you." I go mad. I turn fast and pull her close to my face. I kiss her. My lips and her lips. My tongue and her tongue.

My underwear feels weird. It's wet. I'm wet.

We stop for a second. We look at each other. We don't smile, we just stare at each other. We get lost in each other's eyes, lips, looks.

Frieda jumps down from the counter. She puts her arms over my shoulders. My arms around her waist. We kiss again. And again. And again. Our tongues dancing together.

She pulls away from me. She smiles and then whispers, "You made me wet." I don't know what to say, but I know how I feel. I'm wet too. I smile and go back to kiss her. She says, "No, not here. Come on."

Frieda takes my hand and leads me out of the

kitchen. Then, by the door we see Soledad with an empty glass. I wonder how long she's been there. Frieda asks her, "Sole, you OK?" Soledad nods and leaves. I wanna go after her, but Frieda holds my hand tight. I think, *She'll be OK, this is* my *night*, and follow Frieda to Tracy's room.

I follow Frieda to Tracy's bed.

I follow Frieda. I don't know what to do, but she does. I follow Frieda.

Tracy's Party, Part 3

When we get back to the party, everyone is gone but Soledad, Gina, Tracy, Ikaika, and the boy he was talking to. Paul is his name.

Soledad is sleeping on the sofa. Jane is gone. Gina is lying half asleep on the carpet. Tracy and the boys are taking shots of vodka and eating cold pizza. We sit down with them to eat. We talk and talk and talk.

When the sun comes out we help Tracy clean

up the living room and we all get sleeping bags, blankets, and pillows and sleep on the carpet. I take Soledad's shoes off and cover her with a blanket. She's sleeping like a baby. I ask about Jane, but no one knows. Tracy lies down next to Gina. Ikaika and the guy each take a sleeping bag, they lie next to each other.

The sun is out. Frieda says she has to get home. She kisses me goodbye and leaves. I fall asleep on a sofa, a big smile on my face.

MAY 4TH NIGHT

I had sex. I had sex for the first time and it was wonderful. Sex is wonderful. Frieda is wonderful. Sex with Frieda is wonderful. I don't wanna shower, I wanna keep her smell on my skin.

CHAPTER NINE
ohana

M AY 5ᵀᴴ
 I overslept. Grandma was yelling, "You're gonna be late for school." She was mad, but nothing could erase my smile. I am so happy. I ran to school thinking I am officially a *Māhū* who just had *aikāne*.

Yes, *aikāne*, remember? It means same-sex relationship.

M AY 5ᵀᴴ AFTERNOON
 At lunch I asked Soledad about Jane, but she changed the subject. She asked me if Frieda and

I did it. I couldn't say no, but at the same time I didn't wanna say yes. I didn't wanna upset her.

Soledad's Investigation into My Sex Life

Soledad: Come on, you can tell me. It's not like I'm gonna get mad. I am sorta dating Jane now. Tell me.

Me: First tell me about Jane. She went with you to the party and then she disappeared, what happened?

Soledad: Nothing. Let's say it was a lovers' fight. Now, tell me about Frieda.

Me: Oh, you saw us, didn't you? Making out in Tracy's kitchen.

Soledad: Well, yeah, but what happened after that?

Me: What do you think happened?

Soledad: Just say it, Mikala, say it.

Me: Are you OK, Sole? Are you upset?

Soledad: Of course not, I'm just curious, did you guys have sex or not?

Me: Well . . .

Soledad: Come on, Mikala, aren't we friends? Don't we tell each other everything?

Me: I know, I know.

Soledad: It's OK if you didn't, there's nothing to be ashamed of. There's nothing wrong with being a virgin.

Me: I'm not ashamed, and for your information I am not a virgin. Not anymore, anyway. I did have sex with Frieda. Twice.

Soledad looked at me, surprised. I guess she expected me to say no. She simply said, "Oh." The bell rang and she hurried to leave. She picked up her tray and I asked her if she was OK. "Yeah, yeah, I just gotta run to class. Don't wanna be late to Chemistry again," she said.

And she left. Is it me or is Soledad getting weirder and weirder? She really is not over the fact that

Frieda likes me. I wonder what happened between her and Jane.

M AY 6ᵀᴴ NIGHT

I didn't see Soledad after class yesterday. She hasn't replied to any of my texts. I wonder what's going on.

On the other hand, Frieda and I texted all afternoon.

She says *The Julie Ruin* will be playing at this small club in NYC in a couple of weeks. Do I wanna go? Of course I wanna go. I love Kathleen Hanna.

Frieda: You do? Oh, that is awesome.

I wanna ask her if we are dating or what, but I don't dare. Also, at some point I gotta tell her that my grandparents don't know I'm gay. I know she'll understand it, I mean, every lesbian or gay kid goes through the same thing with parents, right? I bet she's out with her mother, her father, and her stepmother. She seems very comfortable with herself.

P.S. Soledad just called me. I was worried. She's OK, she's just been busy.

MAY 7TH AFTERNOON

Soledad skipped lunch today. Yesterday she told me she's been too busy with this chemistry project. I offer to help her, but she said, "No need." I'm glad everything is cool. I dunno why I felt otherwise. Soledad is cool. I'm sure she's happy for me.

MAY 7TH NIGHT

List of Things to Do Tomorrow

- *Be good at home so,*
- *My grandparents give me permission to go out so,*
- *I can go shopping, and*
- *Get a nice gift for Grandma, and*
- *A t-shirt for me.*

MAY 8TH

Ikaika and I are going shopping today, it's becoming our thing, to shop together. We are getting gifts; Mother's Day is this weekend. It's an odd day, you know, because of my relationship (if you can call it that) with Luana. But every year I get something for Grandma. She raised me, after all.

Ikaika says that he has news to share. I bet it has to do with the guy from the party, Paul. I hope Ikaika's love life is moving forward.

Just like mine.

MAY 8TH AFTERNOON

Ikaika has been accepted to two universities in California!!! Isn't that great? He will be going away in the fall. I'm gonna miss him. He's become part of my life now. He says I should apply in California too, so we can live together as "husband and wife." He's nuts.

We were daydreaming about a wedding in which

he gets to wear the gown and I the tuxedo when my phone rang.

It was Luana. I thought about not answering, but Ikaika took the phone out of my hands, answered, and then turned the phone over to me.

She called just to see how I was doing. (OK, Reader, she had been calling, only I didn't answer. I didn't tell you about it, don't get mad.) I asked her how she's doing (first time I actually did that). She told me she's been organizing an event at a women's shelter in Honolulu. She told me about it, she explained that she's been there for a couple of years now. We didn't talk about the summer. She asked me about school and stuff. And, you won't believe this, she asked me if I was dating someone. I didn't know what to answer.

She said, "Mmhh sounds like you're thinking about it. It's OK, you don't have to tell me anything, but if you're ever up for a girl-talk, I'm here."

I can't help but smile. I kinda feel bad, because she'd been trying for a while, but it's nice that no matter what, she kept trying. She didn't give up. I'm glad Ikaika made me take her call. To be honest, I think I feel almost happy.

Luana, my mother, is trying, really trying. Finally.

M AY 11TH

Mother's Day. Grandpa and I made lunch. We made some mahi mahi with pineapple salad. It was delicious.

We are all having green tea when the house phone rings. I answer. It's Luana. She says hi to me and then asks me to put Grandma on. I pass it to her without saying, "Happy Mother's Day."

Anyway, Grandma and Luana start talking. Then Grandma goes silent for a couple of minutes. She starts crying and yelling. Grandpa stands up, his face worried. Grandma says, "She wants to take Mikala. Luana wants to take Mikala." Grandpa takes the phone from Grandma and yells at Luana to leave us alone.

I don't know what to do. I am too much of a

coward to say something, but at the same time, it's *my* mother they are talking about. *My* life. The weird part is that I'm turning eighteen soon—so nobody can really "take" me, even if they wanted to. Drama.

Grandpa hangs up. He looks at me. I look at him. We say nothing, but everything is out in the open. Minutes run heavy on us, each of us looking for the right words. I go first, I say it, I finally say it: "You know how much I love you and Grandma, but Luana is my mother. I wanna see her. I wanna be with her."

I let them be. I look at them for a minute, trying not to cry, trying to stay firm in my words. I walk away.

The phone rings and rings again. They don't answer. But I do.

Me: Hello?

Luana: Mikala, is that you?

Me: Yes.

Luana: My little girl, I'm sorry, I'm sorry for everything, I'm sorry I haven't been there for you. I hope it's not too late. I want, (she is crying) I want us to get to know each other.

Me: My grandparents don't want us to, they're mad at you.

Luana: I know, they have a right to be mad. It will take some time, but if you let me, I will work my way through it with them. Parents and grandparents—it's love that moves them, after all.

Title: OHANA MEANS FAMILY

ACT I

BLACK.
We hear a woman yelling.

INTERIOR OF A HOSPITAL.

Bright lights. Blue sheets. Nurses and doctors moving around. A young man holds the hand of the woman on the bed. She is sweating, she is in pain.

Doctor (Off Screen): Are you ready to push, Ailani?

Close up of the young woman. She looks at her husband, then nods.

Doctor (Off Screen): Nurse, we're ready. Hanu, you hold your wife's hand.

Hanu (Off Screen): Yes, Doctor.

Doctor (Off Screen): OK, Ailani, now push, push, and let's bring that baby to the world.

Close up of the young woman yelling as she is pushing. Her husband holds her tight. His sweaty face goes from fear to surprise.

Doctor (Off Screen): It's a girl, it's a beautiful girl. Ailani, you did great.

Hanu: Did you hear that, Ailani? We have a girl! We have a beautiful baby girl.

Nurse (Off Screen): Do you have a name yet?

Ailani: Luana, her name will be Luana, because she will be a very happy girl.

Close up to a collection of photos of Luana. Luana as a baby, Luana as a young girl. Luana as a woman, carrying a baby of her own.

Mikala: Luana was a very happy girl, a very happy teen, and a very happy woman. The only problem is that her happiness also meant the sadness of everyone around her.

MAY 11TH NIGHT

Tell me what you think of my script. Be honest, Reader. See, I re-read it and, I dunno, it's strange, but I kinda like it. So far I've only been writing stupid shorts. This is different. I can tell. Maybe this can become something else.

Dialogue with Grandparents about Luana

Grandma just came into my room. I asked her if everything was OK, and she shook her head. She told me this was the worst Mother's Day ever.

Grandma: So, Luana has been sober and clean for two years now.

Me: I know, she told me so.

Grandma: And she wants to take you. She wants you to live with her in Hawaii for your senior year.

Grandpa joined us in my room. He sat down on the bed next to Grandma. He has the same look, as if they had both been crying just a minute ago.

Me: Yes.

Grandpa: How do you feel about that?

Me: I don't know, nervous. But excited at the same time.

Grandma: You gotta understand, it's hard for us. We want to protect you. You are the most important thing in our lives.

Grandpa: We cannot force you to do anything, but please see things from our point of view. Luana . . . your mother, she has made many mistakes.

Me: I know.

Grandma: Yes, I know you do. But your mother, sweetie, she risked your life.

Grandpa: And we don't want anything to happen to you.

Me: I know, but . . .

Grandma: Let's give it some time. Let's see if she is really ready for you. Maybe she becomes a mess again and it will break your heart. Or put you in danger.

Me: What if she doesn't? What if she's finally straightened out her life?

Grandpa: We'll see, we'll see. We can't forget about the many times she would ask for money after telling us that she was sober. Too many times to count.

Me: Did she ask for money this time?

Grandma: No, she didn't. This time she sounded serious about it. But . . .

Me: Well, it's a good sign that she didn't ask for anything, right?

Grandpa: Well, she did ask for something, didn't she Ailani?

Grandma: Yes. She asked for *you*. You know she

wants you. She wants us to help her get to you; she wants you to give her a chance. But you gotta understand, this is very difficult for us.

Me: What does that even mean? This is about *me*, not about *you*.

Grandpa: Mikala's right, you're right. Let's give all this some rest. It's been too much for one day.

Both my grandparents kissed me on the forehead and left. "We love you," they said. Before they left I told them the same words they shared with me so many times, "We are *Ohana*, we are a family, all of us. Luana, you, me." They left with tears in their eyes.

I cry. I can't stop crying.

MAY 11ᵀᴴ NIGHT
To avoid thinking about this whole thing between my grandparents and Luana, I am working on my poem, which I have to submit on Tuesday. I think I will add a dedication, and of course it will

be for Frieda. Last week's events have surely been an inspiration.

Possible dedications:

- *To Frieda and her French Vanilla skin.*
- *To Frieda*
- *To Frieda, a map I want to discover.*

But I really couldn't work on my poem. Instead, I took my phone and started dialing Luana's number. I have decided I wanna learn to be a daughter, just like Luana is learning to be a mother. I have decided to open up with my mother and come out to her.

M AY 12ᵀᴴ
Dear Reader, I came out. I came out to Luana. I came out to my own mother. I talked to her for hours. I told her about me; I told her I am a girl who likes girls. I told her how I don't dare to talk to my grandparents about it, how I am afraid of hurting them by doing so.

And Luana . . . my mother, she heard me, she heard every single word I had to share before giving her opinion. She was crying when she said, "Thank you for sharing this with me. I feel blessed. I am very proud of you. I know I don't know you, but I think you are so brave."

Me? Brave?

She told me she understood my being afraid of hurting them, but she added something important which ended up being kinda funny. "Whatever you do or say, it can't be any worse than what I did when I was your age. Don't feel rushed to do it. Do it when you feel you are ready for whatever they might say. I'm sure it will be odd for them, but both of them are generous, loving people. And they love you more than anything, more than anyone."

I felt kinda bad, it's like Luana was admitting that her parents love me more than they love her. It can't be easy to take that. She told me about her friends in Hawaii. She has two friends who are a couple. They work with her at the shelter.

Luana: They remind me of your grandparents.

You know how they still cross the streets holding hands?

Me: Yes, that's right, they do that.

Luana: Well, my friends do exactly the same, as if they're helping each other, protecting each other, leading one another.

Me: Wow.

Luana: The only difference is that these are two men I am talking about, and one of them is way chubbier than your grandpa.

That made me laugh.

When I hung up with Luana, I felt happy, confident. I opened my document in my computer and started working on my poem. At first, I couldn't write it, but I started a new one, using Miss Moore's idea of playing with a famous poem. I used *One Art* by Elizabeth Bishop and wrote about my own coming out art.

Now I think that this poem should not be dedicated to Frieda, but to the-woman-who-gave-me-life-and-is-my-mother.

CHAPTER TEN
say aloha

MAY 13TH AFTERNOON
Reader, Reader, Reader, today was a great day! Today is the day I became a poet.

See, I had creative writing, and before the class started I handed my poem to Miss Moore. She scanned through it. "It's an appropriation," I told her. "I know," she said. I went to sit down, and then she called me. She asked me if I dared to read it at the end of her lecture. I said yes.

Miss Moore discussed the Beat Generation, then we read a few excerpts from Kerouac and Ginsberg. (Have you ever read them? Those dudes were really something.)

Before the class was over she told everyone she had asked me to share my poem. She said that as a *poet* I was doing an experiment between imaginary and autobiography, just as the authors that we read today did.

I stood up and read my poem. From time to time I took a glimpse at my classmates . . . Oh, Reader, they were all attentive. They weren't giggling or anything.

When I finished they all clapped. Miss Moore had tears in her eyes and thanked me for sharing such a personal moment.

The bell rang, everyone left. Everyone but Soledad, who said, "Now, can I have a copy of your poem?"

I joked and said, "Before I'm famous?" She rolled her eyes. I gave it to her.

MAY 13ᵀᴴ NIGHT

I can't stop thinking about today. About *my* poem. Reader, I honestly think that reading it to the class meant officially coming out, at least with my classmates. I can't lie, I wanted to, it meant a step in my life.

Now, are you ready? I am sharing my poem with you too. (If you want you can first read Elizabeth Bishop's "One Art." Just Google it.)

Coming out
By Mikala Kekoa
Based on "One Art," by Elizabeth Bishop

The art of coming out is hard to master;
so many things seem filled with the intent
to be out that their out is a disaster.

Come out, just a little bit every day. Accept the fluster
of judgmental looks, the years badly spent.
The art of coming out is so hard to master.

Then practice coming out farther, coming out faster:
truths, and loves, and who it is you mean

to be. None of these will bring disaster.

I came out to my mother. And look! my last, or
next-to-last, of three loved words came to me.
The art of coming out isn't that hard to master.

I came out first to myself. And, vaster, to
some people I love, two friends, a teacher, a girl.
I came out to them, and it wasn't a disaster.

—Even coming out to you (your joking voice, your funny
gestures I kinda love) I shan't have lied. It's evident
the art of coming out is not too hard to master
though it may look like (Write it!) like disaster.

MAY 13TH NIGHT

Later tonight I am meeting Frieda, translation: we are chatting tonight.

I wanna tell her about my poem and about next Saturday. It's my birthday and my grandparents are throwing me a small dinner party.

Don't let me forget to tell her about the situation at home, you know, the "blind to queerness" my grandparents possess.

MAY 13TH MIDNIGHT

Frieda is in the closet. Just like me. Surprise, surprise.

We chatted for so long. We talked about each other's families and situations. Frieda's parents divorced because her father started cheating on her mother. Then a few years later he married Frieda's stepmom, who has two daughters, but her stepsisters study abroad. "How very Cinderella of you," I said.

She said, "Not at all, they're cool. I tell you I'd be better off living with Dad. Mom and I just fight all the time." Frieda told me her mother drives her crazy. I don't know how you see it, Reader, but to me Frieda is overreacting. I know, I know, who am I to say anything about mothers and daughters? But still.

P.S. I still don't know if we are dating or what. But I don't feel like asking anymore.

M AY 14TH

My birthday is in two days, but we are celebrating on the seventeenth. Today, my grandma told me about the goodies.

Menu for Mikala's Eighteenth Birthday

- Cucumber salad
- Egg rolls (Grandpa's specialty)
- Grilled Shrimp Skewers (with pineapple and cherries, of course)
- Rum-glazed spare ribs
- Mai Tai cocktails

Oh, and get this: Grandpa told me they have a big surprise prepared for me. I hope it's an iPhone, 'cause mine is dying.

MAY 15TH

Soledad is acting weird again at school. I told her about my dinner party on Saturday and she was very *whatever* about it. All she talked about was this boy she's been sexting with. I said, "And Jane?" She looked at me, shrugged and said, "I dunno, I don't care." She's driving me nuts. I miss the old Soledad. I miss us.

If there is one person I can talk to about what's been happening in my life, it's Soledad. I know I also have Ikaika, but he's been too busy to meet me lately.

I only have you, Reader, 'cause . . . you're still there, right?

MAY 15TH NIGHT

Ikaika texted me, he asked if he could come by. "Look who finally remembers he has a girlfriend," I said. He didn't laugh or anything. He simply said, "So, can I come over? I gotta talk to you." I told Grandpa that Ikaika was coming, you know how grandparents can be about your "boy-friend" visiting you on a school night, but tomorrow is my birthday, so they didn't say anything.

M AY 15ᵀᴴ Very Late at Night
OhmygodOhmygodOhmygod.

Ikaika

is

coming

out.

He's made up his mind about it; he's talking to his parents as soon as the semester is over.

Dialogue of Ikaika's Decision about Coming Out

Me: Does this have anything to do with this new man in your life?

Ikaika: Who?

Me: The guy you met at Tracy's party.

Ikaika: Paul? No, not at all. There's nothing

serious between Paul and me. I think we're just like you and Soledad, at least the way you guys were before Frieda came into the picture.

Me: Oh, so, why are you coming out, then? I thought you were afraid to do it.

Ikaika: Because I can't continue lying. I have to stand up for myself.

Me: But Ikaika, what's the point? See, you'll finish high school in a couple of weeks. After the summer, you'll be going away, and then you'll be able to do whatever you want without your parents knowing about it.

Ikaika: I know, believe me I know. But I can't continue like this. I can't keep lying.

Me: You know you can count on me no matter what happens with your parents, but the truth is that I don't want you to come out. I know this might sound selfish but you coming out will raise questions from my grandparents about the true nature of our relationship, and I don't want that.

Ikaika: Yes, yes, I know. That's why I'm talking

to you now, so you know before I actually do it. It will affect us both, but we gotta, Mikala.

Me: I was starting to like this make-believe affair we have. It made my grandparents so happy. I know, I know I have to come out to them too, but you know, "The art of coming out is too hard to master."

MAY 16ᵀᴴ MORNING
Happy Birthday to Me

Grandma made her special pancakes, with nuts and bits of chocolate. Grandpa gave me the new iPhone I wanted, and now I'm off to school. They told me to be home right after school, because they have a surprise for me.

I thought the surprise was the iPhone, I wonder what they're planning.

MAY 16ᵀᴴ
Mikala's Birthday

It's seven twenty. Mikala walks to school while

reading all the beautiful words her friends posted on Facebook for her birthday. She also reads this long, loving email from Frieda. Things are better after that weird talk about Hawaii and mothers and the future. More and more, Mikala feels that things between them are going great. She'll ask her to be her girlfriend soon.

After school, Mikala arrives at her house, but before she inserts her key in the door, it opens.

Surprise! Luana is right in front of her. Her arms open. "Happy Birthday, Mikala," she says.

Mikala doesn't know what to do. She exchanges looks with her grandparents. Her grandma comes to her side and whispers, "Go ahead, hug your mother." But Mikala is frozen.

This is what she wanted, wasn't it? To see her mother, and now, she doesn't know what to do, what to say. She just looks at her. She is breathless. Luana. Luana is here. Her mother is here.

Luana looks different. Her hair is not shaved, or crazy long, or full of crazy colors. Her hair is just brown and normal, a few grays here and there. No *makeup, no mini skirts. Luana is wearing capris, a pair of Tom's and a long white shirt. She looks like one of those tarot ladies from the flea market.*

Mikala takes a step. Luana takes a step. They look at each other. Luana says, "It's OK if she doesn't wanna hug. She's a big girl now." Mikala doesn't know what to do. She had no clue this day would actually come, especially since the day her grandparents banned Luana. But now, here they are, giving Luana a chance, this is happening. Ohana *is happening.*

Mikala can't take her eyes off Luana. Luana stands closer, she caresses Mikala's hair and says, "You are so beautiful, I can't take my eyes off you. I am sorry I missed all these years of your life."

Tears. Lots of tears.

MAY 16TH NIGHT

So. Luana is here, Reader.

This is the moment. Now that she is by my side, this is when I should talk to my grandparents, just come out. Come on Mikala, "The art of coming out isn't too hard to master."

May 17th Noon

Luana and my Grandma went to the supermarket to get stuff for my birthday. Grandpa and I are moving furniture and getting everything ready for tonight's dinner with my friends.

I've been calling Ikaika. He is the one person I wanna talk to, but he doesn't reply. Soledad doesn't either; her phone's been busy for hours now. She's probably sexting, cybersexting, or something like that. It's my birthday and I have no one to talk about it with. (I know, I know, Miss Drama Queen.)

Wait, I have **you**, that's right. I have you, Reader, but you can't talk to me, can you?

May 17th Night

Summary of a Dinner-Party That Turned into a Nightmare

1. *Every one of my guests came, even Soledad who*

hadn't really confirmed she was coming (and when you get to the end of this you will also wish she hadn't come).

2. *Everyone brought gifts or cards: Tracy, Gina, Ikaika, Soledad, Frieda.*

3. *It was odd to introduce Luana to everybody. I practiced it in my mind a couple of times. "Guys, this is my mother." "Guys this is Luana; Luana this is everybody." "Have you met my mother?" "Have you met Luana?"*

4. *I ended up saying, "Hey, guys, this is Luana, my, you know, mother." Luana said, "Hi everybody, I am her you know mother." It was funny. She made things go smoother. Then Grandma went, "Oh, this is Ikaika, Mikala's boyfriend." Everyone's eyes snapped to me.*

5. *Stupid me, I never told them about this thing between Ikaika and me. Only Soledad knew. I guess they got it somehow. I did tell them I wasn't out with my family. Frieda seemed*

uncomfortable though. My mother was giving me the eye. She mouthed, "Boyfriend?"

6. *Soledad and Frieda started talking, I guess she's explaining the whole thing to her.*

7. *I was kinda hoping that after dinner was served, the adults of my family would go away or something, but no, they stayed there, telling stories about Hawaii.*

8. *Luana kept an eye on me and Ikaika.*

9. *I kept an eye on Frieda and Soledad.*

10. *"Let's get the cake," Luana said, and she and Grandma went to get it. Grandpa went to get the candles.*

11. *I sat down next to Frieda and apologized for not telling her about this charade between Ikaika and me. She said, "It's OK," but her "OK" was the kind of "OK" that everybody knows translates into, "It's not OK, at all!"*

12. *Soledad became Frieda's PR or something. She said, "What Frieda doesn't understand is what exactly is going on between you and*

Ikaika?" Frieda added, "That's not what I said."

13. Soledad and I started to argue. "Come on Mikala, you can't expect us to believe that there is really nothing going on between you and Ikaika. You two are bi, aren't you?"

14. Luana and my grandparents came back to the dining room singing "Happy Birthday."

15. Everybody sang "Happy Birthday."

16. Everybody clapped.

17. Everybody said, "Make a wish."

18. Everybody clapped again, as I blew out my candles.

19. Soledad touched Frieda's shoulder, whispering something to her.

20. I got mad.

21. I got very mad.

22. Luana and my grandparents went back to the kitchen with the cake, to cut slices and serve on plates.

23. *Soledad and me argued. Frieda stayed on the side, quiet.*

24. *"This was your idea," I told Soledad. "Yeah, because you wanted to stay in the closet," Soledad said.*

25. *And then . . .*

26. *Soledad opened her purse, took out a folded piece of paper and started reading my poem, my coming out poem. How did she get it?*

27. *My grandparents and Luana heard the poem. They looked at me. They looked at Frieda. They looked at Ikaika.*

28. *I took the poem from Soledad's hands and slapped her face. "Get out of my house!" I yelled. She didn't leave. Frieda did, though.*

29. *"Mikala, sweetie, what's all this about?" Grandma asks.*

30. *Ikaika said, "You gotta tell them. You gotta talk to them, Mikala." Then he told everybody, "I think we should all leave." He turned to my grandparents and added, "Mr. and Mrs. Kekoa,*

I am very sorry, Mikala and I never meant to hurt you."

31. *My grandparents were silent. Luana started caressing my back, as if bracing me for a possible fall.*

32. *I heard Ikaika tell Soledad, "How dare you? What's your problem?" If Soledad said something, I didn't hear her. All I saw was her trying to keep it together.*

33. *"Mikala, talk to us." Grandma said.*

34. *"I, I'm sorry," I said.*

35. *I ran to my room and locked myself in.*

36. *I opened my diary and started writing to you. Reader, I'm stupid, I am so stupid.*

JUNE

For you, it's one day, one hour, or one minute since you last read my words. But it's been weeks since I dared to come back to this diary. I don't even know what day it is. I just know that today is our last day of classes. The last few weeks have been so shitty. My grandparents are not talking to me. Frieda is not talking to me. I am not talking to Soledad. The only person at home that talks to me is Luana, only I don't really talk to her. I just "yes" and "no" to her from time to time.

But overall I'm fine, or at least, I'm better than Ikaika. He's been kicked out of his house. He's been staying with Tom-Tom, his ex. They are not back together, but Tom-Tom was the only one who offered Ikaika a place to stay. His plans? Find a job during the summer and then go to California as planned.

If things hadn't happened the way they did, maybe my grandparents would have allowed him to stay with us. You see, the problem here is not that they found out about me being gay, but the fact they *found out*, the fact I *lied* to them for so long, including about my relationship with Ikaika.

Grandpa kept staying they didn't raise me to be a liar. Grandma said nothing. She just stays in her room all day long. I understand and I don't understand. I mean, think about it, I already told you all the things Luana did in the past, and now she's forgiven. Me? I just didn't open up to them about my sexuality and I am shunned.

It's not fair. It's not fair.

Then there's Frieda, she just won't pick up the phone and she unfriended me on Facebook. Who knows what Soledad has been telling her? I'm sure she's all over Frieda now. Fucking Soledad, to think that she was my best friend, and then this.

I feel like shit. I cry all the time. I hate myself for writing that poem. I hate myself for being the way I am. Stupid queerness.

JUNE

Luana and I have been hanging out, or whatever you call it when you go out and talk with *the woman who gave birth* to you, the woman *you are starting to call mother*. She agrees with me, she thinks my grandparents are overreacting, but at the same time, she reminds me that they haven't done anything but love me all these years. I owe them time to heal, she says.

Dialogue between Me and Luana My Mother

Luana: Mikala, believe me, if it hadn't been for them, who knows what our lives would have been like, yours and mine?

Me: I know, I know, believe me. And I did my best to always be a role model student. I never did any of the things you did. Oh, I probably shouldn't be saying that, right?

Luana: No, you're right. I know that. What you did doesn't compare to what I did to them throughout the years, but I guess with me they knew what they were going to get and with you, well, they probably had different expectations.

Me: But . . .

Luana: Wait, let's just be clear about one thing. They are not mad at you for being gay, they aren't like that. Miki, no one knows them like you, they are the most loving, understanding parents in the world. The problem is . . .

Me: That I lied.

Luana: Yes, for a long time, and you involved other people in it.

Me: But it wasn't even my idea to date Ikaika.

Luana: I know, I know. But they don't see it that way.

Me: And you, you lied so many times. I just lied this one time.

Luana: Yes, I did, but they forgave me, didn't they? I'm here right now.

Me: Well, yes, but look how many years it took them to do so.

Luana: No, sweetie, if it took this long, it wasn't because of them.

Me: I don't understand.

Luana: Listen, it didn't take *them* years to forgive me, it took *me* years to realize the problem was *me*, it took me years to ask for their forgiveness. When I got cleaned up, and came to them, and really asked to be forgiven, they forgave me right away. You need to talk to them, open up. Trust is very important to them. You did not trust them about . . .

Me: My queerness.

Luana: About you, period. Listen. My summer break is almost over, and I will have to go back to Hawaii soon. Why don't you come with me, just for a few weeks? It will distract you, and give them a chance to figure things out. When you come back, you can all sit together and talk things out.

Me: So, you're going back to Hawaii?

Luana: Yes, I have to. Why?

Me: Can't you stay?

Luana: I wish I could, but I have a job there. A job that matters. For me, it's a big deal to be reliable, to finish what I started there.

Me: Wait, you're really inviting me? You aren't just saying it?

Luana: No, of course I'm not just saying it. I want you to come. Maybe if you like it, you can stay with me.

Me: In Hawaii?

Luana: Yes.

Me: What about school?

Luana: There are schools there.

Me: What about Grandma and Grandpa?

Luana: We can say aloha to them.

Me: Say goodbye to them? Are you nuts?

Luana: Oh, Mikala, there's so much for you to learn. *Aloha* doesn't *only* mean hello or goodbye. It also means peace, compassion. It means love.

J ULY
Reader, it is happening, it is really happening! Let me explain. Luana and I are flying to Hawaii next weekend. I have sat down with my grandparents, we had a long conversation. I cried. They cried. I asked them to forgive me. They asked me to forgive them. "Maybe we demanded too much from you," said Grandma. I told them this was not their fault. I told them I just didn't know any better.

Then Luana told them she was taking me with her to Hawaii. "At least for the summer, and we'll see what happens from there . . . " My grandparents and I exchanged looks. Grandpa said, "Is this what you want?" I nodded.

J ULY
I am excited and sad and nervous. I feel so many things at the same time. Ikaika says he saw Frieda hanging out with Gina and Tracy a couple of days ago. Soledad wasn't there. No one has seen her. I sometimes feel the urge to call her; she was my best friend, after all. I wanna know why she did it. Luana says I shouldn't. "Just say aloha, life goes on."

I guess she's right. I should just treasure that I had a chance to have her in my life; in the end, if it hadn't been for Sole I wouldn't have met Ikaika or Frieda. Or you. Let's not forget, Reader, that Soledad brought us together; she's the one who made me write.

I started this diary as a way to help someone understand queerness, but that someone ended up being me. I am accomplishing my goal, I am learning what being queer is, and soon I will be in Hawaii. I do not know where my life will lead from there, but that's the fun of it, right?

Aloha, Reader.

Aloha, aloha.